"Tell me more about your dream,"
Emma probed

"Well, I stood there while the blonde tore off my clothes. The brunette just lay back and watched. I was getting pretty hot by then with all the tempting and teasing—"

Emma's pencil snapped. She jumped and stared down at the stub left in her hand.

"Take it easy, Doc." Nick laughed. "I haven't even gotten to the good part yet."

She took a deep breath. "Are you sure this was a dream?"

He seemed momentarily disconcerted. "What? You think I made this up?" He moved closer and slipped his hand around her waist. "Doc, you wound me. I thought we were getting to be...close." He lifted her chin and leisurely trailed his lips down her neck.

She moaned softly. "Nick, this isn't right. If the study were over—"

He captured her mouth with his, her eager response fueling such a raging desire it made him so hard he throbbed.

"Doc, I think the study is going *just fine....*"

Blaze™

Dear Reader,

I hope you're half as excited about the new Blaze line as I am. As soon as I heard about Blaze I knew I wanted to write one. Ideas started popping into my head, and before I even got the thumbs-up, Nick and Emma were born. *In His Wildest Dreams* became as real to me as my three cats that love waking me up at five-thirty every morning to be fed. You'll see one of them make his debut in this story, only his name has been changed to protect the not-so-innocent.

My hat is off to the dedicated Harlequin Toronto crew whose very hard work has made Blaze possible. It's gutsy, sophisticated and sexy, and I'm proud and pleased to be on board.

See you all between the pages!

Debbi Rawlins

P.S. Check out Blaze online at www.tryblaze.com!

Books by Debbi Rawlins

HARLEQUIN DUETS
46—THE SWINGING R RANCH
46—WHOSE LINE IS IT ANYWAY?

HARLEQUIN AMERICAN ROMANCE
808—HIS, HERS AND THEIRS
860—LOVING A LONESOME COWBOY

IN HIS
WILDEST DREAMS

Debbi Rawlins

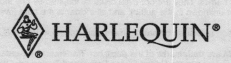

HARLEQUIN®

TORONTO • NEW YORK • LONDON
AMSTERDAM • PARIS • SYDNEY • HAMBURG
STOCKHOLM • ATHENS • TOKYO • MILAN • MADRID
PRAGUE • WARSAW • BUDAPEST • AUCKLAND

Special thanks to Brenda Chin and Birgit Davis-Todd
for giving me this opportunity.
And to my new editor, Susan Pezzack,
for making the transition so seamless.
You guys are the best!

ISBN 0-373-79017-1

IN HIS WILDEST DREAMS

Copyright © 2001 by Debbi Quattrone.

1

"BULL. HE'S NOT on a conference call. He's watching the Lakers game. Tell him it's Nick Ryder and to get his butt on the line." Nick adjusted the phone between his jaw and shoulder, leaned back in his sister's office chair and got comfortable.

On the other end of the line, the temp hemmed and hawed for a moment. Nick sighed, taking pity on her. If she'd been his financial planner's regular secretary, she would've laughed, told him the latest dirty joke she'd heard, and then patched him through to Marshall.

"Just tell him I'm on the line, okay?"

"All right, Mr. Ryder, one moment please."

He squinted out the apartment window, hoping he'd see Brenda coming down the street. When he saw no sign of her, he cleared a spot between the two stacks of student papers she was grading and swung his feet onto her desk.

"What the devil are you doing calling me in the middle of the game?"

Nick chuckled at his friend's gruffness. They went way back to prep school days, followed by Yale. After graduation, Marshall had stayed for another two years of graduate studies, but Nick couldn't wait to get the hell out, and he had. Not because school was hard, but because it was too easy. The curriculum bored him silly.

"By your pleasant tone I take it I'm winning our bet?"

"One of these days, Ryder, you're going to fall on your ass."

Nick snorted. "Tell you what, without even asking the score, I'll give you another four points."

"Smug bastard."

"Man, that's what I get for practically giving you your money back?"

Marshall's laugh was interrupted by a cough, and Nick winced. He wished the guy would quit smoking like the doctors had advised. "What do you want, Nick?"

"I got a tip on a new restaurant chain. Their stock is about to go up and I want five hundred shares before it does."

"You know restaurants are risky."

"Yeah, but I've got this hunch."

Marshall sighed. "Far be it from me to underestimate one of your hunches. No matter what, you always manage to land on your feet."

"What's life without a few risks?"

Marshall muttered something Nick didn't hear. Just as well. He was sick of the "Golden Boy" cracks, even though he knew Marshall didn't begrudge him his good fortune. Not like some of the other guys they'd gone to school with.

Was it Nick's fault that he'd never had to study for exams, that he was lucky at the track, that at twenty-nine he'd invested well enough to have made close to a million, or that he didn't have two kids and a nine-to-five job?

He wasn't foolish. When it really counted he believed only in calculated risks that bred success, and once he'd thrown in, he stayed committed to the end. Not understanding the odds ended in failure. Nick made it a point not to fail. Not professionally, or personally.

He passed on the restaurant stock info and was hanging up when he heard a key in the door.

As soon as his sister stepped inside, her gaze flew to his booted feet. "Off the desk. How many times do I have to tell you?"

"Look." He raised his boots a couple of inches. "I'm using a coaster."

Brenda shook her head, a smile lurking at the corners of her mouth. "What are you doing here anyway?"

He got up and took the pair of bulky brown grocery sacks from her arms. "I need to talk to you."

"I gave you a key for emergencies."

"This definitely qualifies as an emergency." He carried the sacks into the kitchen, and then pulled out a package of chicken. "The freezer, or the fridge?"

"The fridge." She started unloading the second sack. "You could have called."

"It's easier to invite myself for dinner this way."

"What?" Brenda slid him one of her amused glances that annoyed the hell out of him. "No date?"

"Tiffany has to work late."

"You're actually dating someone who has a job, *and* takes it seriously?"

"Pathetic, isn't it? I keep telling her there's more

to life than sticking her knees under a desk eight hours a day." He yanked out a bag of salad greens and made a face. It was a funky mix of wild greens—weeds if you asked him—that Brenda favored but made him gag. "Disposal?"

"Try it, Buster."

He tossed it in the vegetable tray, and then took out a beer. "So what's for dinner?"

"How do you know *I* don't have a date?"

"Yeah, right." He uncapped the bottle. "Want one of these?"

She sighed. "That hurt."

Nick stared at his sister, puzzled by her sullen expression. "Come on, Bren, you know what I meant. You're always working or studying for your doctorate. It's not that you can't find a date."

She gave him the silent treatment for almost a minute, long enough for him to start feeling like a heel, and then she grinned. "Gotcha!"

"Brat." She was two years younger but definitely more mature, or at least more serious about life, mostly because he refused to grow up. No fun in that.

"We're having chicken and pasta." She ducked around him to get to the spice rack. "If you'll get out of the way and put some water on to boil."

"Yes, ma'am. Oh, before I forget, you had a call...someone named Emma. She had to cancel lunch tomorrow. Her last subject bailed out on her. She said you'd know what that meant."

"Oh, no." Brenda set aside a jar of garlic salt, her expression crestfallen. "I can't believe this. Did she sound really upset?"

"Kind of matter-of-fact, I guess." He rooted

around a lower cabinet until he found a large pot. When he stood, Brenda hadn't moved, her expression still troubled. "Who is this woman?"

"A friend."

"That much I figured out."

"I mean a really good friend. She's saved my butt a couple of times during midterms. She's incredibly together, kind of like I want to be when I grow up."

"Like that's ever going to happen."

That got him a tiny smile. "Look who's talking." Then she looked bummed again.

"Hey, cheer up. Your friend will figure it out."

"Yeah, I know. It just doesn't seem fair. Her thesis is on dream interpretation, and she's been working hard at it for over a year now."

"Ah, another one of your perpetual student friends."

"Knock it off, Nick. Emma's different. Things haven't been easy for her. She doesn't have parents who paid her tuition. She was on partial scholarship and had to take out a student loan, plus she works part-time as a waitress *and* as a teaching assistant for Professor Lyster."

Nick yawned.

"Sometimes you're a jerk."

"What? It's my fault Grandmother's trust fund paid our tuition? I didn't hear you complaining."

Brenda glared at him. "You could show some compassion."

"For God's sake, lots of people put themselves through school. What's the big deal?"

"Yeah, but Emma's different. She's had to work

twice as hard because of a learning disability she had as a child.''

He stuck the pot under the tap and started to fill it with water. ''How much am I supposed to put in here?''

When she didn't answer, he turned to find her staring out of the window, totally lost in thought. Her chin-length dark hair hid most of her face but he could tell by the slump in her posture she was really upset.

He turned off the water. ''Hey, Bren, why don't we go out for Chinese, or maybe Italian this time? My treat.''

She shook her head and gave him a wan smile. ''Nah, I don't feel like it.'' She went back to preparing the chicken. ''What did you want to talk to me about?''

Ah, hell. Rotten timing. Of course Nick didn't think Brenda would have a problem with doing him this small favor, especially since she'd been too busy studying the past few years to use the family ski house, but still. ''I need the Aspen place for Thanksgiving.''

A small frown drew her brows together. ''It's my turn to have it this year, right?''

He didn't like the way her interest suddenly piqued. ''You're not planning on using it.''

''Why shouldn't I?'' She had that lost-in-thought look again. It made him nervous.

''You haven't been there in five years. You don't even like to ski.''

''But it's nice and quiet out there. An excellent place to unwind, study, whatever.''

"It's quiet here."

She glanced at him with that faintly amused look again. "What's the deal? You promised some sweet young thing you'd take her skiing in Aspen?"

"So?"

"So, too bad. It's my turn to have the house. You should have checked with me first."

He muttered a curse. "Bren, come on."

"Sorry, Nick, I really am." She did look apologetic, as though she wasn't going to give in. Dammit. "But I do need it this year."

"Bull. You hadn't even remembered it was your turn."

"I know, but this thing with Emma..."

Oh, man, there was that apologetic expression again. "What does this Emma have to do with it?" He paused, struck by inspiration. "If you think she might be upset, shouldn't you stick around and comfort her? You are her friend." He tried to look sincere and concerned. Too bad Bren knew him too well.

Her look of disdain made him sigh. "Why don't you rent another place?" she asked, turning back to cutting up the chicken.

"Are you kidding? Everything's booked by now." He took a long pull of his beer, annoyed that everything had gotten complicated. "Hey, how about I rent you a place? Anywhere you want. Jamaica? St. Thomas? You and your friend can soak up the sun and study to your heart's content."

She pursed her lips, drummed her fingers on the counter. Good. Obviously she was thinking about it. "I have another solution."

"Okay." He started to relax.

"You can be Emma's subject."

"What?"

"You let her study you for the next two weeks and the house is yours."

"That's no solution, that's blackmail."

"Suit yourself." She shrugged and turned back to the cutting board, but not before he saw the beginning of a grin.

"*Study* me? Like figure out what's going on in my subconscious?"

"Not exactly. You simply relay your dreams to her and she analyzes them, and then compiles the data for her thesis."

"Using a bunch of psychobabble." He snorted. "That is so not going to happen."

She shrugged again, the stubborn glint in her eye all too familiar. She meant business.

"What if I find someone else?"

"Nope. You're perfect for the study. You can fall asleep in a heartbeat and you're good at recalling your dreams. Besides, she needs someone yesterday."

"Oh, man." He abandoned the pot and sat at the kitchen table. "I can't just drop everything for the next two weeks."

She laughed. "Like what? Playing tennis, or maybe having dinner with your girlfriend du jour?"

He sighed with disgust.

"Like I said, suit yourself."

"How many hours a day does this thing take?"

"You'll have to talk to Emma about that."

He narrowed his gaze in suspicion. "You aren't trying to fix me up with her, are you?"

"Oh, God no. Emma's much too good for you."

"Thanks."

"Don't mention it. Just let me know if I should call and tell her to expect you."

"You realize this is blackmail."

Brenda smiled. "I call it a trade."

He got up, muttering a few choice words as he headed out of the kitchen.

"What about dinner?"

"I don't have time. Call your friend. Tell her she's got a new sucker."

Brenda waited until he was out of sight and then pumped her hand in the air. "Yes!"

She did a little victory dance around the kitchen table, and then headed for the Mickey Mouse phone Nick had given her last Christmas.

This was just perfect.

EMMA SNOW STRAIGHTENED HER BACK, squared her shoulders and looked Jake straight in the eyes. "Would you like to go to Dean Sutter's reception next month? Um, that is, with me?"

Jake looked back blankly.

"Wait, let me try that again." She flipped back her ponytail, and cleared her throat. "Next week Dean Sutter is having his annual reception for the students who are completing the graduate program. If you aren't doing anything...what I mean is...would you like to go with me? As my date. Well, not really a date of course...just someone to sit with at dinner."

Jake stared at her a moment longer, yawned and then walked away, clearly unimpressed.

She glared at his retreating back. "Thanks, you ingrate. See if I bring home any more kibble."

He didn't even turn around. Instead he gave her "the tail." She was fairly certain it was the feline version of flipping her off. The persnickety tabby often turned and stiffened his tail when he was displeased about something.

"I heard they're serving salmon for dinner," she called after him, but he ignored her and disappeared down the hall.

Emma sighed. She didn't know why she was going through this futile exercise anyway. If she didn't complete her thesis, she wouldn't be going to the reception. Which meant she'd be stuck in school for another several months, assuming Professor Peters's patience didn't run out. Or her funds did. Both were serious contenders to screwing up her degree.

God, she had to be the oldest graduate student in history. She sank onto the edge of her bed and dropped back onto the mattress and stared at the chipped ceiling. Of course that wasn't true—many people returned to school after raising families or whatever, but it felt as though she'd been in the graduate program forever, lagging behind because money had run out, or her job as a teaching assistant required too much time, or her mother was calling her back home to Utah for some ridiculous reason.

Emma fell for it every time, no matter how flimsy her mom's new excuse. Guilt would start gnawing at her for not having been the perfect child her parents had dreamed of having, and she'd drop everything to go be her mother's crutch. Usually even without her mom's subtle reminders of how much she'd sacrificed to work with Emma, the years she'd spent helping her learn to read so she could be a "normal" child.

She blocked the destructive thoughts from her mind. Her energy was much better spent finding a new subject for the final phase of her thesis, not that she honestly had much hope. It had taken her best Bob Seger CD, a nerve-wracking dinner with the lascivious Martin Stanley, and a promise to clean Norman Cove's apartment for two months to secure the last three male subjects.

She sighed. Now that Norman had backed out, at least she didn't have to scrape together a few hours a week to do his cleaning. Time was becoming more of an issue. As it was she didn't know how she could continue to volunteer at the animal shelter.

She loved working with the strays. It was a way of giving back for the kindness her elderly neighbor had shown her when she herself had been a kind of stray, roaming the neighborhood after school when she'd felt unwelcome in her own home.

There was a bright side. Not having to clean Norm's apartment would allow her time to work an extra shift at the pub. Or more time for her thesis.

If she still had a shot.

She was so screwed.

The phone rang, and Emma leaped off the bed, foolishly hoping someone was answering her new ad from the library bulletin board.

"It's Brenda," her friend said before Emma finished getting out her hello. "How you doing, kiddo?"

"Better than roadkill."

"That good, huh?"

"I can't believe this is happening." She carried the phone back to the bed and flopped down. "I am so pissed at Norm I could strangle him."

"Why did he bail?"

"He claims he's flunking chemistry and he has to use the time to study more." Emma snorted. "Flunking my butt. I got a glimpse of his new lab partner."

"What a jerk! He's a whiz at chemistry. Did he actually think you'd buy that excuse?"

"Hard to believe he beat a million other sperm to the finish, isn't it?"

Brenda laughed.

Emma joined her, and then sighed. "Men. If they put one on the moon, they ought to be able to put them all there."

"No argument from me." Brenda hesitated. "This isn't like you to be joking at a time like this. You're not going over the edge on me, are you?"

"I think I'm in shock. I'm so close to finishing—this is like a bad dream, no, a nightmare. If I don't find some humor, I'll do something—I don't know what, but it won't be pretty."

"Well, you can thank me with a hot fudge sundae because I'm about to save your butt."

"What? You're going to dress in drag and be my final male subject?"

"Are you ready for some good news or not?"

"I am so ready."

Brenda paused dramatically. "I've got a guy for you."

Emma frowned. This had better not be one of Brenda's setups. Although it seemed she'd given up trying months ago. "Define that further."

"My brother."

"The womanizer?"

Brenda cleared her throat. "That's not exactly how I'd categorize him. Women are drawn to him."

"You said once he had a different 'flavor' for each week." Emma stared at her pathetically short fingernails. At least she wasn't biting them anymore. Maybe they'd look halfway decent in time for the reception.

"I know, but not because he necessarily encourages it." Brenda sighed. "Nick's one of those guys women do silly things for...even the ones you'd never expect to behave like that act like brainless morons around him."

Emma rolled her eyes. "And you want *me* to go out with him?"

Her friend laughed. "Oh, God, no. He's volunteering to be your test subject."

Heat singed Emma's face. She knew she was bright red right now, a curse of her fair Irish skin. "I knew that."

Brenda chuckled. "I wouldn't do that to you, Em. He's my brother and I love him...I even like him most of the time. But I would never try to fix you two up. Trust me."

"I'd been thinking about the Dean's reception and my mind was on a different track so I—" Emma's muttering came to an abrupt halt as realization sunk in. "He'll do it? For the whole two weeks?"

"Yup."

"Why?"

"He owes me a favor."

Emma got a funny feeling in her tummy. "Does he *want* to do it?"

"No."

"Great."

"Have any of your subjects wanted to do it? If I remember correctly, you did an awful lot of bribing and bartering."

"True, but this is the end of the line. He can't bail out on me because he has something else to do, or decides he doesn't like being asked a gazillion questions."

"He won't bail. We have an understanding."

Emma hesitated, not that she had much choice. As she'd said herself, it was the end of the line. Heaven help her if she didn't finish her thesis. Not only was she flat broke, but the job they'd promised her at the clinic would be given to someone else who already has their master's. "Does he have any time restraints?"

"I doubt it. He does some day trading on the Internet, some charity work, and he just got over his hobby of tinkering with old cars. He doesn't have a regular job."

Emma thought hard, trying to remember what Brenda had said about her brother. All she recalled was that he'd been a gifted student, who hated school but parlayed his genius into a small fortune. And that he was a real charmer with the ladies.

Good thing Emma was immune to that kind of stuff. Sex was overrated, in her opinion, media hype, advertiser's bait. One encounter had been enough to satisfy her curiosity.

She switched the phone to her other hand, and then flipped through her calendar. "Does he know we'll have to get started right away?"

"He knows."

Her pulse started speeding with renewed hope. Brenda knew how important this was to her. She wouldn't volunteer her brother unless she felt confident he'd see the study through. "I'd like to get started tomorrow."

"He'll be there."

"I owe you a hot fudge sundae. Hell, I owe you twenty of them."

"Forget it. My thighs can't take it." She sighed, and then paused. "Em, don't let Nick get to you, okay?"

Emma laughed. "Afraid he might charm the pants off me?"

Brenda laughed, too. "You're right. I don't have to worry about you. Besides, you aren't even his type."

Emma winced. She knew her friend didn't mean anything by that remark but it still smarted. Guys had never been attracted to her, not like they were to other girls. She'd been too busy studying to date, and the only boys who had asked were bookworms and nerds, too.

"Okay, this is for sure and I can go ahead and reserve the lab for tomorrow afternoon?"

"It's for sure," Brenda said. "What time?"

"I'm working the lunch shift tomorrow, and if you don't mind skipping our coffee date, we can start at three."

"No problem. I'll tell him."

"Let me know if that time is okay with him."

"It will be."

Emma frowned. Brenda sounded awfully smug. "You didn't do anything illegal to get him to volunteer, did you?"

Brenda just laughed.

2

TARDINESS WAS ONE of Emma's two major pet peeves. She muttered a couple of choice words as she fumbled with the key and finally unlocked the lab door. She bypassed her desk and hurried to the back room, more an oversized walk-in closet than anything else, and dropped her backpack on the small refrigerator they kept full of soda to ease the long hours of lab work.

Only she and two other graduate students used the place but there was so much personal junk stowed between the two metal filing cabinets anyone would think an army of students lived here. While she prized neatness, she overlooked the mess the others left. She understood how so many long hours working in the lab stole time and energy.

What she didn't understand was how everything could have gone to hell at the pub in a matter of minutes, and at the end of her shift, too. Of all days for Manny to knock a tray of drinks out of her hands, and then take off for the beach before he helped her clean up. Of course everyone else disappeared, too, even the bartender.

She started to undo her coat and gritted her teeth when she split a nail on the second button. Was she ever going to be elated when she could finally quit that awful job. In more ways than one. She looked down and made a face at the ridiculous red, satin teddy-like thing she had to wear, and then shrugged off the coat and tossed it onto a file cabinet.

If the tips weren't so damn good she'd tell the owner what he could do with this skimpy excuse for a uniform. But no way could she find another job for the same amount of hours that paid her tuition and rent. It was a sorry reality that some women were forced to make their living that way, but she was glad she wouldn't be one of them for long.

If everything went well with this final study, she figured she could hand in her resignation in about a month. Bless Brenda's heart for however she bribed her brother to fill in.

Nick was perfect for the study in two ways. According to Brenda, he had amazing dream recall, and second, he had time. Brenda had told her once how he'd been a quiz kid who made his fortune early, and then diverted his energy to women. Good for him. All Emma cared about was that for two weeks he was all hers.

Other than that, she knew little about him, which was terrific for the study because she'd approach his dreams with few preconceived notions. It would have been better that she knew nothing about his reputation as a charmer. But that wouldn't be a problem...not professionally, and certainly not on a personal level. Those kinds of overconfident guys were a turnoff.

"Ouch!"

Another nail bit the dust as she shimmied out of the skin-tight uniform. She threw it aside, adjusted her thong panties, which she'd never in a million years have bought except she needed them to accommodate her uniform. Much to her surprise, she'd ended up liking the fit and bought several more.

She glanced at her watch as she reached for her khaki pants, and groaned. He'd be here at any minute. Her bra...where was her bra? God, she hoped she'd remembered to bring one.

NICK LET HIS PORSCHE IDLE a minute before he turned the ignition off. The temptation to peel out of the parking lot was so great he knew if he didn't cut the engine now he just might head for McGillycuddy's pub and forget all about this crazy dream analysis stuff, and Aspen.

But man, he didn't want to disappoint Tiffany. Because when Tiffany was happy, she was amazing.

He got all hot thinking about her and quickly stepped out into the cool North Carolina afternoon air. The single-story white stucco building he faced was old and not much to look at, but of course, this wasn't the main campus...more like an annex for the science department where the labs were located.

Pocketing his keys, he slid a glance around the small parking lot. A handful of white sedans, nondescript, unimaginative, were parked perfectly within the lines. He'd bet his bank account each and every one belonged to a professor.

Nick exhaled sharply. Just being on campus, any campus, gave him the creeps. Academia had to be life's greatest penance. He couldn't believe his own sister actually *wanted* to be a teacher.

He adjusted the collar of his black leather jacket, patted the pocket where he'd dropped his keys. Okay, he could do this. It was only for two weeks. Aspen was worth it. Tiffany would be very happy.

It was a long walk to the door. Only about twenty yards, but with lead feet it was a tough trip. When the front door wouldn't open, he almost turned back around. Maybe he should knock.

He tried the knob again, and hell, this time it opened.

He cleared his throat, and then stepped across the threshold. The room was clean but shabby. A metal desk was crowded into the corner, the top covered with stacks of files, yet managing to look uncluttered. Beside a black leather lounge chair was an intimidating and sophisticated piece of equipment. The wire tentacles were obviously some kind of probes and he quickly looked away. Better not to think about it.

Other than three mismatched metal file cabinets, not much else was in the room. Including anything breathing. Maybe he'd luck out yet.

There was another door that had to lead somewhere, and in good conscience he figured he ought to at least check for signs of life. He moved in that direction and saw her.

At least the back of her.

And she was naked.

Nick froze.

He tried to back up, get out of view, but his gaze stayed glued to the brown silky hair that hung nearly to her waist—a slim waist, that dipped in nicely above a curvy, firm-looking behind. And legs…man, she had some wheels.

Nick swallowed, but his mouth was too dry. If he

didn't get the hell out of here, he'd probably start coughing.

She angled to the side to pick up a piece of clothing and the last thing he realized before he bolted out the front door was that she'd been wearing a thong. A red, silk one. Thongs did scary things to his heart.

He managed to close the door softly behind him, and then stood in the cool air and broke into a sweat. She couldn't be Emma Snow. Not from what Brenda had told him about the woman. Emma was a serious student, determined to complete her thesis, had no social life, no interest in dating or men in general, and was totally off-limits to him—as if he'd be interested in someone like her.

So who was this woman? Another student, or test subject? A friend of Emma's maybe?

After checking his watch, he decided to give her another five minutes before knocking. The extra time wouldn't hurt him either. His physical reaction needed to settle down.

Another couple of minutes and he heard someone moving around inside. He adjusted his jeans, and then knocked this time.

The door opened immediately. A brunette wearing oversized black-rimmed glasses smiled at him. "Nick?"

"Yeah." He tried to look past her. The other woman was obviously still in the back.

"Come on in. I'm Emma." She waited until he got inside and then offered her hand. "I can't tell you how much I appreciate you filling in like this."

Her hand was small, fragile, but her handshake was firm. He gave her another look. Hazel eyes, clear skin, no makeup. The only outstanding feature was her lips. Naturally pink and full enough they looked cosmetically altered. But indulging in vanity didn't fit the profile Brenda had given him.

Her general appearance did. The outdated glasses and tight bun at her nape made her look older than she was. In grade school they would have called her a bookworm, and a few other less flattering names.

"If you'll take a seat at the desk I have some paperwork for you to fill out," she said, gesturing to a battered gray fabric chair. The back was high and the numerous pills looked as though a cat had used it as a scratching post.

"What kind of paperwork?" He moved closer to the back room door and tried to get a glimpse of the other woman. No luck. "This is all confidential, right?"

"Of course. Any information you give me is strictly for the purpose of the study." She smiled, and his gaze riveted to her mouth. Her lips and her friend's legs. Now there was a combination to be reckoned with. "But I don't think you'll find I'll be asking anything too personal. This basically asks statistical information."

"And then what?"

"I'll explain what we'll be doing for the next two weeks."

He took the seat at the desk and stared down at the questionnaire. Innocuous enough questions, but this part he'd expected. It was her poking around his psyche, trying to figure out what his dreams meant that he dreaded.

It wasn't anyone's business. Not even his, as far as

he was concerned. Dreams were dreams. They didn't mean a damn thing. Merely something to do while you slept so you wouldn't get bored.

"I'll be in the back getting set up. Let me know when you finish filling that out."

"Hey." He waited until she turned around. "You said this is all confidential, right?" She nodded. "Nobody else will be here."

"Not a soul."

"What about now? Anyone back there?" He gestured with his chin toward the back room.

"Nope. It's just us."

He frowned. So where was the mystery woman? Maybe there was a back door. Or maybe...

He gave Emma another once-over. Baggy khaki pants, a white lab coat over a navy-blue cotton shirt. Hard to tell what she really looked like under all that stuff. He doubted she'd be wearing a red silk thong, though. Not this woman. And the hair...it couldn't be that long and fit in that small tight bun.

"Any other questions?"

"Let me get this straight." He took another furtive glance toward the back. From what he could see, the room looked really small. "This is just going to be you and me. No one else is involved."

Her gaze narrowed with concern. "Look, I really appreciate you doing this, but if you have any reservations that might prompt you to drop out mid-study, I need to know now. I can't afford the time to look for someone else."

Man, he'd give just about anything to take the opportunity to bolt. But anything didn't include the Aspen house. Hell. "Nah, I'm okay, Doc, just a little nervous about you finding out all my deepest, darkest secrets.'' He gave her his most winning smile.

She frowned. ''We'll talk more after you've filled that out.''

Emma hurried to the back room. She hoped he took a while to complete the questionnaire because she needed time to regroup. Her sudden imbalance had little to do with him, of course, or that he was supposed to be some kind of lady-killer. Frankly, she didn't see it. Running late always made her a little nuts. That was her problem.

Granted, there was something appealing about him. Nothing blatant, nothing even easily identifiable. Sure, his thick dark hair was attractive in a messy, touchable sort of way, and he had a disarming smile that could probably melt many a resolve. But so did a lot of other guys she knew.

Except his face had character, from the crinkly lines fanning out from the corners of his dark eyes, to the small moon-shaped scar over the left side of his upper lip. A small chip marred otherwise perfect teeth. Clearly he wasn't vain or driven by perfection, or he would've had these minor flaws fixed.

Her uniform lay in a heap where she'd left it in her haste to get into her street clothes. She gathered them up, stuck them in a bag to add to her laundry and then checked her hair. It was a mess. She'd misplaced a couple of bobby pins and her usual bun was a little wobbly, but it would do.

After waiting a couple more minutes, she went out to check on Nick's progress. To her surprise, he'd already finished and was talking on her phone.

''Let's have Chinese tonight,'' he said just as she

walked in. Although he hadn't seen her yet, his voice lowered. "I'll leave dessert up to you." His laugh was husky, sexy, and then he looked up and saw her. "I have to go. I'll see you at eight."

Emma sighed, pitying the poor sap on the other end who fell for his sad lack of originality. "Did you have any questions about the paperwork?" she asked as soon as he'd hung up.

"Nope."

She paused a moment, waiting for him to get out of her chair. He didn't. If anything, he leaned back and got more comfortable, so she took the visitor's chair facing the desk and turned the questionnaire around to face her.

After a quick perusal she looked up to find him staring at her. She cleared her throat. "I'll give you an overview of what we'll be doing in the next two weeks."

He grimaced slightly.

Her stomach tightened. "If you have a problem committing to two weeks—"

"No." He shook his head, his expression agitated. "I just—go on."

God, she had a bad feeling about this. But Brenda had told her not to worry. Nick had his faults, but backing out of an agreement wasn't one of them. She sure hoped Brenda was right.

"I don't know how much you care to know about the theories upon which I'll be basing my interpretations—" There was that wince again. "What?"

"Nothing." His expression was sheer innocence. "I'm listening."

She hesitated a moment, tempted to call him on his

obvious negative reaction to their conversation. But on the other hand, did she really want to hear what he thought? Did she want to give him an opening to withdraw from the study?

She took a deep breath and began again. "There are many misconceptions about dream interpretation and I thought it might be helpful if I cleared some of them up before we got started."

He didn't look happy, but at least he hadn't bolted. He glanced toward the back room, and then gestured with his hand for her to continue.

She leaned back in her chair and wondered what he found so fascinating in the back room. Had he seen the mess her associates left? "There's significant research indicating that dreams reflect our real-life concerns and are helpful in coping with conflict or solving problems. I operate on this theory."

He stood suddenly. "You're not psychoanalyzing me, Doc. No way. No how."

"First of all, I'm not a doctor. Yet. Secondly, I have no intention of trying to psychoanalyze you or anyone else." She exhaled sharply. "Could you sit down? You're making me nervous."

He muttered a mild oath, shrugged out of his leather jacket, and then tugged at the neckband of his T-shirt as if it were too tight. "Yeah, right."

"Would you let me finish?"

Eyeing her with distrust, he lowered himself back to the chair as he tossed his jacket to the side. "Brenda told me there wouldn't be any psychobabble involved."

Emma bristled, but she kept her cool. "This is a

science. Not psychobabble. And like I've already assured you, anything discussed here is confidential."

"That's the thing, Doc." He ruffled his hair in a gesture of frustration. "Every time you remind me this is confidential, I get a rash."

Her gaze flew to his arms, his neck, any exposed skin.

"Figuratively speaking, of course," he added. "Exactly what kind of questions are you gonna ask me?"

It took her several seconds to realize he'd spoken to her. His plain white T-shirt stretched snugly across his chest. Every muscle group was nicely represented. His arms weren't too shabby either. Firm, rounded biceps strained against the hem of his sleeves.

"Doc?"

"Stop calling me that." She quickly met his gaze. He seemed bewildered. Thank God he didn't know she'd been ogling him like a silly teenage girl.

"Why not? You're going after your doctorate, right?"

"Ultimately."

"So, start acting the part."

"That's called fraud."

He drew his head back, clearly surprised. "No, it's not. You have a vision of who you want to be. Fake it till you make it. You'll get there faster."

She frowned, not quite grasping his point, but both fascinated and irritated with his new authoritative demeanor. "May we get back to the study?"

"I'm serious." He leaned forward, resting his elbows on her desk. "What I'm talking about is a perfectly legitimate way to attain a goal. It's the same principle as when job counselors tell you to dress for the job you want, and not the one you have.''

It was easy to understand why he'd achieved success early. His solemn tone of voice, and the intensity in his eyes gave her a glimpse of the man who'd been driven to succeed. What an intriguing side to him.

She tapped her pencil on the edge of the desk. ''The study?''

''Sure.'' He grinned suddenly, and leaned back, looking totally relaxed. ''Doc.''

There it was.

That subtle indefinable quality that drew women to him like ants to a picnic. Was it his slightly mischievous grin?

Or was it the way his gaze held her captive, as if telling her he wasn't going anywhere, and neither was she. Amazing really, how the attraction crept up before you knew what hit you.

Luckily she was able to respond in a strictly professional, scientific manner. She cleared her throat, checked her bun. ''Okay, where was I?'' she mumbled, her voice still sounding a bit creaky, so she cleared her throat again. ''Oh, yes, my method and theories.'' She was back in control, unmoved, untouched by the darn devil in his eyes.

''I won't lie to you, I believe that dreams reveal important facets about ourselves in metaphorical forms. They show us how we feel about others, about our relationships, and about ourselves, for that matter. They help illustrate our hopes and fears and weaknesses, and as an interviewer and interpreter, I will be pointing out—'' She stopped, frowned. ''What are you doing?''

"Huh?" He raised his gaze to hers. "Go ahead. I'm listening."

"No, you weren't. You were—" She brought a hand to her mouth and futilely felt around for anything foreign. God, there was probably something stuck in her teeth.

"Okay, so you caught me." That devilish grin again. "Did you know you have perfect lips?"

She squinted at him, certain she'd heard incorrectly.

"Perfectly shaped. Perfect fullness. Perfect shade of pink. You should be doing lipstick commercials."

"Mr. Ryder, I don't think—this isn't the time or— just knock it off."

"What?" His eyes widened in genuine surprise, and then he nodded with annoying understanding. "I embarrassed you. I apologize. However, I only meant it as a compliment." His lips curved in that smile. "Besides, you caught me staring."

"You didn't embarrass me." Right. Heat singed her cheeks and she knew they were redder than an August tomato. "But I would like to stick to the business of the study."

He threw her a questioning look, and then shrugged. "Of course. I didn't mean to distract you."

The hell he hadn't. She stared down at her notebook so she wouldn't glare at her subject, piss him off, and then have to go beg and barter for a new one again.

"As I was saying," she said, slowly, each word deliberate, "I believe dreams do tell us a lot about ourselves, and I will of course, interpret the information you give me, but ultimately only you will know what each dream means to you.''

He snorted.

"Excuse me?"

"Nothing."

"You always make rude noises for nothing?"

Amusement lit his dark eyes, and his mouth started to curve in a slow smile. "Sorry, Doc, I didn't mean to rile you."

"Right," she muttered, and stared down at her notes. They weren't really notes. Just something to look at while she collected herself.

How could this guy be so charming and annoying at the same time? The laughter that seemed to spring to his eyes was the irritating part. As for the rest of him...

Well, he did have a great chest and shoulders, broad, muscled without being in-your-face. And though Emma couldn't honestly remember being impressed by a man's hands before, she found herself periodically studying the way his long lean fingers restlessly, silently tapped the desk. That in itself wasn't remarkable, but they inspired a sudden erotic image of him caressing her breasts that about knocked her over.

She took a deep breath. What was wrong with her? Having lustful thoughts about a virtual stranger was not her style. Especially not one who could make or break her thesis.

"Are we done here, or what?"

Nick's impatient voice broke into her preoccupation, and try as she might, she couldn't do a darn thing about the flush that crept up her neck and ripened her cheeks.

"Tomorrow we'll get started," she said calmly. "So it's important that you record anything and everything you remember about tonight's dreams."

"Sometimes they're a little X-rated." He smiled. "Is that a problem?"

Great. "Record everything."

"Everything," he repeated with a devilish look in his eyes.

"Every last detail you recall."

"Okay, Doc." He managed to make the two simple words sound like a threat. "You got it."

God, she hoped he wasn't talking about some heavy-duty sexual fantasies. For the sake of the study it would make the data both interesting and thorough, but good golly, what a torturous two weeks for her.

She shuddered mentally, and then caught him staring toward the back. She followed his gaze. "What is it you find so fascinating?"

Something that looked like guilt flickered in his eyes as they met hers. Just as quickly it vanished. "Keep any prisoners back there?"

"Only ones who give me attitude."

"Oh man, Doc, you're getting me excited."

She sighed. Obviously keeping this one on track would be a challenge. "Brenda said you have excellent recall. Do you use any particular method or trick?"

"I read an article that suggested giving a title to a dream as soon as you remember any part of it."

"Does that help you recall more of the dream as the day goes on?"

"Yeah, I think so. If it was a good dream, and my mind wanders back to it during the day, it seems to unfold more."

"Excellent. Keep a notebook with you."

"Right. Record everything." His voice and expression turned grim. He started to shrug into his jacket, and Emma forced her gaze away from the way the muscles played across his chest. "So, we're done?"

She closed her notebook. "Yes." She hadn't even skimmed the surface, but maybe it was better he wasn't so curious about her methods and theories. He was skittish enough. "Unless you have any questions."

He shrugged, pulling a pair of sunglasses out of his pocket. "Same time tomorrow, or do you want to get this over with earlier?"

Gee, such overwhelming enthusiasm. "It'll have to be the same time as today. I don't get off work until then."

He nodded absently, looking distracted, before he walked out the door without another word.

Emma waited a minute before she used the shiny base of the engraved brass stapler she'd received as an award to look at her reflection. Of course her image was slightly distorted, but still, her lips looked pretty normal to her. She pursed them. Maybe a little fatter than most, but...

"Hey, Doc."

At the sound of Nick's voice her heart nearly exploded and she straightened, almost flinging the stapler against the wall. "Yes?" Remarkably, her voice was intelligible.

His brows drawn together in a puzzled frown, he seemed too absorbed in his own curiosity to have noticed her vanity. "I do have another question." She nodded, and with his gaze narrowed he asked, "Are you sure there isn't anyone else here?"

Geez, talk about paranoid. "Positive."

He sent her a skeptical look, and then a lazy mysterious grin curved his mouth. "Okay, Doc, have it your way. For now."

3

HOW THE HELL had he let Brenda talk him into this? Nick checked the rearview mirror to see if anyone had entered the deserted parking lot. Okay, so he was early and the doc had probably just gotten off her shift. He'd have to remember to ask Brenda what kind of work Emma did. Not that he really cared but if she was going to be poking around his head, he figured he had a right to know something about her.

He stared down at the notes he'd taken from last night's midnight romp. Here he'd purposely instructed himself not to dream and he'd ended up having a couple of doozies...about naked women with long dark hair, long legs and silk thongs.

Shit!

He glanced at the rearview mirror again and this time an older, beat-up white sedan chugged into the parking lot. Doc was behind the wheel. He couldn't see her face, but he saw the mass of shiny dark hair. Since he was the only one there, he had to suspect she'd seen him, but without any acknowledgment she veered off toward the side of the building and parked out of sight.

A few minutes later, she hurried around the corner, her hair pulled back in a messy bun, the collar of her long tan coat pulled up around her neck. Odd. It had warmed up and wasn't cold enough for her to be wearing a coat.

He continued to watch as she made tracks in the opposite direction, nearly running into the pink azaleas flanking the stark white lab. If she'd seen him, she was pretending she hadn't.

He got out of his Porsche. "Hey, Doc."

She slowed, reluctance in every small jerk of her body as she turned around. "Sorry, I'm running late again," she called out, slightly breathless.

"You're not. I'm early." He closed the car door.

"Give me five minutes, okay?"

"All right if I wait inside?"

She touched the back of her hair, and quickly tucked up a stray. "Um, why don't I make sure things aren't a mess. Someone else used the lab after we did yesterday."

He snorted. "You should see my place."

She looked hesitant, and then he got it. Maybe she had to get her friend out the back door, although why the cloak-and-dagger was a mystery to him.

"Damn, I forgot something." He opened his car door. "Can we make it ten minutes?"

"No problem."

He got into the Porsche and watched her unlock the lab door and then hurry inside without a backward glance. He didn't bother to start the engine, but waited until the door closed before he got out and strolled around to the back.

No one was there. He started to wait but then noticed there was no back door. He kept walking until he'd made a circle around the small building. Only one door. Obviously the woman had still been inside while he met with Emma. But why would she lie about someone else being there? It didn't make sense. Unless Doc thought he'd get testy about the confidentiality issue. That was possible.

He gave her a couple of extra minutes before he went inside with the leather binder of notes he'd taken. She was ready for him, sitting at her desk, her glasses perched on her nose, a notebook in front of her, and a tape recorder set on the opposite edge of the desk, closer to the guest chair. Presumably where he would sit.

Man, everything he said was going to be on tape. Immortalized. They would have to discuss that.

"Have a seat." Those great lips lifted into a tempting smile, and he almost forgot about the tape recorder. "I see you have some notes."

"Man, do I. It's amazing I got any sleep at all last night."

She laughed. "Everyone dreams quite a lot. We just aren't all lucky enough to remember the details."

"Well, Doc, I'm not sure you're going to want all these details." He opened the binder and flipped through pages and pages of writing.

"Excellent." She lifted her gaze to his. "I'm impressed."

"Don't be. You probably won't want all this stuff."

"Are you kidding? This much recall is a gold mine."

He wasn't so sure. "Do I just give this to you, or what?"

She seemed surprised. "No, you have to describe the dreams in as much detail as possible."

"What do you think all this is?"

She gave him a small tolerant smile that annoyed him. "A reminder for you. I promise that as you relate the events of the dream, you'll begin to recall other details. There is nothing unimportant. Once you begin, keep talking. Let it all flow."

Hell, this wasn't going to work. He didn't do "flow."

"What's wrong?" She laid down her pen. "You look distressed."

"Hell, yeah, I'm distressed. You asked me to record all this stuff, and now you want me to go over it again."

She had that tolerant, patient look down to a damn science.

"I know this isn't easy. Dreams seem so personal—"

"Of course they're personal." He slouched in his chair, annoyed and frustrated.

"But you don't have control over them. There's no reason to be embarrassed."

"Embarrassed." He grunted. "That has nothing to do with it."

She tapped her pencil on the desk with hard rapid intensity. Impatience pulled her lips into a straight line. "Let me be blunt. Brenda explained what we needed to do here before you set foot in the lab. What's the problem?"

He glared back at her. Dammit. She was right. "Okay, you want the details. Here are the details…" He set his notes aside. He didn't need them. One particular dream he remembered with so much clarity he still had a hard-on.

"Wait a second." She flipped on the recorder.

"Is that necessary? You have my notes."

She didn't answer him. Just gave him one of those tolerant looks again, and then leaned back in her chair with a pencil in her hand. "Begin whenever you're ready."

Next year too soon? He took a deep breath, exhaled slowly. "I'll start with my first memory," he said, and she nodded. "I was in this—look, it's going to sound weird."

"Don't worry about it. Most dreams do. Go on."

He shifted to a more comfortable position. "There was this room with a bunch of chairs and sofas, almost like a waiting room, except there weren't any people there, only me. Seconds later, women started to parade in, most of them topless. Some of them were big-busted, like really big, like augmented big. The blonde with the tassels started to unbutton my shirt." He paused. "Can I have some water or coffee or something?"

Emma stared at him, wordlessly, and then she blinked. "Of course. I should have asked you before we started."

They both stood at the same time.

Nick motioned for her to sit back down. "Tell me where it is. I'll get it."

She shook her head. "We have colas, orange juice and water. If you want coffee I'll start a pot."

"We?" Now he had her.

"I share this place with two other graduate students and we all chip in to keep the fridge stocked."

Another graduate student. Of course.

"Water's fine." He sank into his seat, and watched

her out of the corner of his eye as she hurried into
the back room.

Well, now that he sort of knew who the other
woman was, he couldn't just come out and ask for
her name and phone number.

Could he?

He sighed. He had his plate full for right now. Normally talking about sex in any form didn't bother him,
but he could tell he'd startled her, which made him
uncomfortable.

To him sex was a game, harmless recreation, but
only if both players agreed and got equally as much
out of it. Nick very carefully stuck to partners who
shared his philosophy. That way no one got hurt.
However, he also understood that not every woman
agreed with his attitude, and he respected their opinions, too.

Unfortunately, his dreams weren't nearly as dis-
creet.

He glanced at the binder he'd set on her desk. It
seemed to take her a long time just to get a glass of
water, and he was tempted to grab his notes and do
some creative editing, maybe clean up the details a
little, omit some of the more colorful parts.

Before he could think the possibility through, she
was back with a bottle of Evian. It sure hadn't taken
nearly five minutes to grab that.

"Anything else before we resume?" she asked, her
finger poised over the recorder button.

"I don't think so."

She made a face at the recorder. "I thought I'd
stopped it. Let me rewind to where we left off."

He took a long cold sip of the water while she

fiddled with the machine. But he nearly spit it out when she stopped and hit play, and he heard his own mutterings. Not of his dream as he'd relayed it to her, but the mild oath he'd uttered after she'd left the room, and then the more damning murmurs expressing his doubts.

Hell, he hadn't realized he'd said anything out loud. Fortunately most of it was unintelligible.

To her credit, she didn't even try to listen. She quickly continued to rewind the tape further. She played the last few seconds to remind him where they'd stopped, and then settled back in her chair, her gaze lowered.

He took another sip of water. "Okay, the blonde undid the top three buttons of my shirt, but she stopped when a redhead came in and told her I wasn't the one. By the way, the redhead had on clothes."

Doc looked relieved.

"The blonde got angry and said she didn't believe her, and then tried to unfasten my next button. The other woman said something but it was in another language, and the others started laughing."

"The other women?"

"Yeah."

"Where were they?"

"Sitting on the chairs or lying on the sofas. Do you need to know whether they had their clothes off or not?"

"Yes." Her tone was crisp, professional, but a faint pink crept into her cheeks.

"All but three of them had taken everything off." At the vivid memory he shifted to accommodate the strong reaction his body was having.

"Were they strangers, or did you know any of them?"

"Never saw them before."

"Sometimes in our dreams people take on different shapes and forms. Did you believe any of these women to be someone you knew...even though she didn't look like she was supposed to?"

He thought for a moment. "No."

She made a brief notation. "How about the room? Did you know where you were?"

"Nope."

"Any other details about it you remember?"

"Not really." He shrugged. "I guess my mind was on the women."

A smile tugged at the corners of her mouth and she pressed her lips together. "Okay, let's get back to the women. What else do you remember about them?"

"The redhead had a bag with her and she started taking out scarves and handcuffs and massage oils. When the blonde unzipped my fly, the redhead didn't say anything. She just kept staring at me while she laid out the stuff she'd brought. But then the blonde reached into my pants to stroke me, and the redhead yanked her hair until she moved back."

He paused for another sip of water. No surprise, he'd gotten harder than a rock replaying the scene.

"What were the other women doing?" Doc's voice didn't sound too steady and her face was getting redder.

He gladly avoided her gaze. "Kissing and fondling each other." When the silence grew, he chanced a look at her. "Shall I leave out that part?"

"There's more?"

He nearly laughed at her scandalized tone. "I'm not your first male subject, am I, Doc?"

"No, not at all."

"Then you know men can have, um, wilder imaginations sometimes."

"Of course." She straightened, pushed her glasses up the bridge of her nose. Her cheeks were still pink, her voice a little high, but her gaze narrowed suddenly, and when her glasses slipped, she looked over them at him. "There is a major difference between dreams and fantasy."

"I know that."

She stared at him in silence for a long torturous moment. "These *are* dreams you're describing, and not wishful thinking, right?"

He chuckled. "Trust me. I would not be describing my fantasies to you."

She blinked, lifted her chin. "As long as we understand each other."

"Look, I'd be happy to edit some of this. It can't all be that important—"

She vigorously shook her head. "That would compromise the results of the study. Tell me everything you remember."

"Okay, Doc, where were we?"

She pressed rewind and kept her gaze on the tape. It took a couple of tries before she found where they'd left off, and each time she had to listen to him describe the dream, her cheeks got a shade pinker.

"There, I think you've got it," he said, taking pity on her, and she immediately stopped the tape and pressed record.

"Okay, so while the other women were kissing,

and the redhead and blonde were arguing about something—''

''About what?''

''I couldn't tell. I don't think I really heard what they were saying but just had a sense they were angry. Anyway, I was too concerned about this other woman who came in.''

''Another one?'' Her eyebrows lifted in shock, and then she quickly wiped all expression from her face. ''Tell me about her.''

''Let's see, she had long dark hair, great legs, a great— I couldn't see her face. I got really agitated about that, but the only view I got was the back of her.''

''Did you feel as though you knew her?''

''Nah, I think maybe I was trying to place her but I really had no idea.''

''What was she wearing?'' She paused, frowning. ''Nick?''

He slumped back. How could he have been so stupid! Through the haze of dawning, he vaguely heard Doc call his name. ''A black thong,'' he said absently. ''That's all.''

The woman in his dream was the same one he'd glimpsed yesterday. That's why he couldn't see her face in the dream. Wow, this was really something. Kind of weird. He'd never obsessed like this before.

''You're remembering something, I take it?''

He stared blankly at her. Should he admit he saw someone else in the back room? She'd have to fess up then. But she'd also have a million questions about the woman being the centerpiece of his dream. No thanks.

"Not really." He shrugged at the curiosity in her face. "Sorry, Doc, I guess I was too excited about, um, the upcoming events to think about anything else."

"Right." Emma fidgeted with the pencil, and then stared down at her pathetic notes. Good thing she was taping this interview or she'd be in sorry shape later. Either the other male subjects she'd studied had held back on her, or this guy had only sex on the brain. Of course the others had relayed some sexual encounters, but Nick was too much.

Part of her was glad for the opportunity to make her study so thorough. The other part wanted to sink into a hole and not surface for a month. It wasn't that she was a prude, but it wasn't easy to sit here and listen to this stuff and pretend it didn't faze her. The last thing she wanted to do was spook him so that he started censoring himself.

On the other hand...

"Did you want me to continue?" he asked casually, as if they were discussing the weather.

"Yes, of course. You were telling me about the dark-haired woman."

"Oh, I didn't forget, Doc." He smiled again, shifted in his seat, getting comfortable, his eyes half closing, probably trying to get back into the dream. *Oh, boy.* "She didn't say anything, just watched the other two women argue. And then it was almost like she communicated to them silently because they stopped suddenly, and the redhead picked up the handcuffs and slapped them around my wrists."

"Wait a minute, let's back up." She was really botching this. She hadn't had him set the scene up properly. "You said you were sitting. Were you restrained in any way?"

"No."

"So you could have gotten up and left if you wanted?"

He drew his head back in exaggerated surprise and flashed a quick grin. "Would you have?"

She tried not to glare. "Go on."

"Let's see, oh, yeah…the redhead cuffed me to these two pole lamps on either side of my chair and then she finished unzipping my pants." He paused, frowning, as though he were trying to recall something.

"Was there anything familiar about her?"

"Which one?"

"Any of them."

"I don't know." He shrugged. "Yeah, maybe."

"I'm not trying to put words in your mouth. Think about it for a minute and see if anything comes to mind."

"Uh, sorry, Doc, but it wasn't my mind they was appealing to."

Emma sighed. "Would you be serious?"

"You kidding? I'm being so serious and honest, it's scary."

She groaned inwardly. She had to give him that one. "What else?"

"The dark-haired woman was just about to turn around but the blonde blindfolded me with one of the silk scarves before I could see the brunette's face. And then I felt all these different hands on me, yanking off my shirt, pulling down my pants."

He paused to take another sip of water, and Emma

braced herself for what came next. "Maybe you should just use my notes for the rest."

She forced her gaze to meet his as she stopped the recorder. "You don't need to be embarrassed."

He leaned back, totally at ease. "I'm not. Actually, I'm enjoying the replay. I figured you might be a little uncomfortable."

She gave her best breezy laugh and shoved her glasses into place. "I've heard hundreds of dreams. I'd hardly be embarrassed at this point."

And then she caught her reflection in the brass stapler. Oh, God. If her cheeks got any redder, Nick would probably think she was having a stroke and call the paramedics.

"Okay, Doc. Have it your way."

She stared down at her notebook, and thought about how many loads of laundry she had to do, how she'd waited too long to defrost her freezer, again. When heat still stung her cheeks, she thought about how she'd already eaten her backup pint of chocolate ice cream and hadn't replaced it. That helped sober her a little.

"Ready?" She started the recorder again without waiting for his reply.

"After they had my clothes off, one started kissing me while another one licked and bit my nipples. I was irritated that I didn't know who they were, and then they both backed off and I remember being cold where the air hit the damp spots on my skin where they had their mouths."

Emma swallowed...mostly to make sure her mouth wasn't hanging open. "So it was important to you to know the aggressors' identities?"

"Do I seem like the kind of guy who'd go for anonymous sex?" Nick grinned with that devilish twinkle in his eyes, and for the first time she could recall, Emma wanted to smack a test subject. "No, Doc, I didn't care particularly who they were. I wanted to know if it was the blonde or the redhead who was sucking me so hard I thought I'd come for a week."

She tried her damnedest not to show any reaction. "I guess you left that part out," she said crisply, attempting to cool her rising temper. He was trying to goad her, she was sure of it.

"Actually, I was just getting to that— Hey, why are you looking at me with malice in those pretty hazel eyes? It's a dream, Doc, I can't help what went on in my sleep. You said so yourself."

"You're right."

"You also told me not to hold back or censor myself."

"Yes, I did." It was difficult to maintain her composure when she truly had the urge to smack that innocent look off his face.

"So why are you looking so pissed off?"

"I'm not pissed off. That would be unprofessional." She pushed up her glasses, enormously thankful they hadn't fogged up. "I'm disappointed that you seem to think this is a joke."

"Not true." He gave his head an emphatic shake. "You may be used to all this blunt talk but I'm not. I have to look for a little humor to ease the tension."

Oh, yeah, she was really used to all this. She cleared her throat as she readied the recorder again.

"I apologize for misjudging the situation. Please continue."

He tried to hide a smile, but she saw it, lurking at the corners of his mouth before he passed a hand over his face and blew into his palm.

She didn't believe for a minute that this talk made him uncomfortable. He'd already admitted that he was getting off on it, and that she believed. Because, dammit, she wasn't making it through this session totally unaffected herself. She'd had to shift twice to make sure he couldn't see how much her nipples had tightened, and how they pushed against her flimsy bra and thin cotton shirt.

"Well, Doc," he said, stretching, his arms wide, his chest broad and muscled under his snug blue T-shirt. "I hate to disappoint you but that's about it. After they got me out of my pants and started—" A ghost of a smile played about his lips again. "Doing 'the nasty,' I woke up. I had urgent business that was best taken care of in the bathroom. But I don't think you need to know about that."

She gave him a disapproving glare in answer, and clicked off the recorder.

He immediately straightened. "We're done?"

"Yes, unless you have another dream you remember." She almost hated to ask.

"You're in luck." He indicated his notes with a jut of his chin. "The next one I call *In Broad Daylight.*"

4

"HOW DID YOUR MEETING with Nick go yesterday?" Brenda had gotten to Big Joe's diner first and was already working on a strawberry milkshake.

"Fine. We had our first session this afternoon."

Brenda switched her interest from the milkshake to Emma. "And?"

"You know I can't tell you what we talked about. If he wants to discuss his dreams with you, that's up to him." Emma stared down at the menu, even though she knew it by heart.

Even though she always got a cup of chicken vegetable soup and a side of fries.

"Oh, no, don't tell me he got to you, too."

That ridiculous crack made her look up. "What are you talking about?"

"I no sooner mentioned his name and your cheeks got pink. What's up with that?"

"That wasn't about Nick." She sighed with indecision and studied the small jukebox on the table. "He has some rather racy dreams. And that's all I'm saying."

Brenda burst out laughing. "Poor baby. I should have warned you. Nick is totally uninhibited."

"Really?"

At Emma's sarcasm, Brenda laughed again.

"That's just Nick. He skipped so many grades in school that from the time he was ten he hung out with older kids. At sixteen he started college. Mom and Dad kind of left him alone because he was such an excellent student, and sometimes he hung around with too racy a crowd. Made him immune. Nothing bothers him. He doesn't mean anything."

"Right." Maybe today she'd splurge and add a chocolate malted to her order.

"Oh, come on, Em. I know him. I give him a hard time, and yeah, I've made cracks about him, but he has a lot of good points. He's loyal to a fault, a real pushover for the underdog and the best listener. If I ever need an ear or sound advice, I go straight to Nick. Honest, he's okay. I wouldn't have offered him up as a sacrifice to your study, otherwise."

"Gee, thanks."

Brenda slurped up the last drop of her strawberry shake.

"Think about it. Would you want to tell a virtual stranger about stuff your subconscious dreams up?"

Emma shifted with unease. No, as a matter of fact, she probably wouldn't. "Yeah, but we all know that most of it is metaphorical for other things that are happening in our lives."

"*You* may know that, but the rest of us just squirm at the vague recollections the next day."

"That's why this study is important. We should be able to use our dreams as messengers from our inner voices. Let the dreams help solve our waking problems. Look how many cultures considered dreams messages from the gods. In the ancient world, countries like Greece and Egypt, dreams were considered the ultimate form of guidance.''

"Don't get huffy. You've got to admit, not all your colleagues agree with that theory.''

"The informed ones do.'' Emma pushed up her glasses. In spite of the fact that she was bone-tired, she'd been in a fairly good mood until a moment ago. "Most scientific theories have opponents. That's why studies are important to prove them.''

"I'm not disputing that, but merely pointing out that a layperson would naturally be a little squeamish about spilling out their midnight mental escapades.'' Brenda's gaze narrowed. "Why are you so touchy today? It isn't like you.''

Emma sighed. Where the heck was their waitress? She needed a malted *now.* "Sorry if I bit your head off. I didn't sleep well. Talk about midnight escapades.''

Brenda leaned forward with interest. "Do tell.''

She didn't get it at first, and then Emma realized her friend wanted to hear about her dreams. To Emma's utter amazement, she almost physically recoiled. The thought of sharing last night's walk on the wild side made her want to run and hide.

Brenda laughed. "Not so easy, is it?''

"It's not that...''

"Yes?''

Bless Callie's heart. The waitress appeared at the perfect time to take their order. As usual, Brenda was indecisive and had to ask for a description of every special. Emma welcomed the brief respite.

She was genuinely startled by her own reluctance to share her dream. Reluctance heck, abhorrence was more accurate. Of course the dream did involve Nick and Brenda might misunderstand. Emma herself still hadn't figured out what her inner voice was trying to tell her. But nor had she tried too hard to figure it out.

The dream was still so real in her head that she could almost feel Nick's hands on her skin, palming her breasts, rubbing her nipples, sucking them. Their session today was going to be a nightmare. She'd have to force herself to concentrate and not drift back to last night's subconscious frolicking.

She came out of her preoccupation just in time to give her order to Callie.

And meet Brenda's expectant gaze. "Well?"

"Well, what?"

"You were going to tell me about your dream."

"Actually, I was going to tell you why I couldn't. I don't remember most of it."

"Emma Snow, I can scarcely believe it, but you're lying through your teeth."

"I am not." It was a little scary how indignant she could get when Brenda was right. Emma was lying through her teeth all right, and she'd hang on to the lie till her dying breath.

Brenda toyed with her straw, a worried frown drawing her brows together. "I hope this isn't about Nick."

"Don't be silly." Emma gasped when her friend tucked a strand of hair behind her ear. "You finally bought them."

"What? Oh…" Brenda touched the diamond stud on her right ear. It had to be at least a carat. "I was still saving up for the suckers. Nick bought them for me. I found the jeweler's box in my desk drawer after he left the other evening.''

"Wow!"

"I shouldn't have mentioned I wanted them. He's always doing things like that.''

"Interesting.''

"You look doubtful." A sisterly defensiveness rose in Brenda's eyes. "I told you he's a nice guy.''

"I'm sure he is," Emma said lightly.

"Do me a favor and don't mention the earrings. He's funny about that. He never gives a gift outright. He tucks it away somewhere for you to find, and then acts like he doesn't know anything about it. It's weird, almost like he's embarrassed.''

Emma smiled. She wouldn't have guessed that about him. "That's actually kind of sweet.''

"Don't be foolish and fall for him. I mean it, Em.'' Brenda shook her head, her eyes concerned. "I love my brother but his idea of a serious commitment is staying the night.''

"Fall for Nick?" Emma laughed. "I'd sooner eat chocolate-covered grasshoppers.''

"THANKS FOR THE EARRINGS.''

Nick finished drying the hood of his '55 Chevy before he turned around. "What earrings?''

Brenda gave him an indulgent smile as she entered the garage and sidestepped the assortment of chrome polishes and car washes he'd left on the ground. "They're exactly what I wanted.''

He shrugged and shook out the rag. "They aren't from me.''

"Then I won't bother to insure them. They're probably fake."

He slid her a sidelong glance. "I begged Mom and Dad to get a puppy instead of a sister. But no, they had to hatch something they could put in frilly pink dresses."

"The luckiest day of your life was the day I was born, admit it."

"In your dreams." *Oh, hell.* He glanced at his watch. He had to shower and shave soon, so he could meet the Doc by four-thirty. "What did you want, Pipsqueak?"

"Nothing. I figured I'd stop by to see how things were going with you and Emma."

He discarded the rag and frowned, disappointed more than annoyed. "Doc told you."

"Huh?"

"What do I care?" Shrugging it off, he picked up one of the polishes and studied the label.

"I have no idea what you're talking about." She snatched the can out of his hand. "Quit ignoring me."

"I'm not. I have to finish this up before my appointment with Doc this afternoon."

Brenda frowned. "Why are you seeing a—" The confusion lifted from her face. "You mean Emma."

He poured some of the grayish-blue liquid onto the torn piece of burgundy towel. "She's not going to be happy with last night's installment."

"Your dream?"

He nodded and started on the hood. Man, this baby could still shine.

"She didn't tell me anything, you know."

Sliding her a glance, he kept polishing. "Wouldn't

matter if she did. I didn't tell her anything I wouldn't tell you.'' He smiled at the thought. ''Theoretically speaking, of course.''

''Yeah, but the point is, she didn't and wouldn't discuss any session she had with you or anyone else. She's not like that.''

He gave her a challenging grin. ''How is she?''

''Ethical...professional...moral. What did you think of her?''

He shrugged, and then put a little more elbow grease into the job. If he got the Chevy looking good enough, he'd pick Tiffany up in it tonight.

''You have to have some sort of opinion.''

''She's okay.''

''That's it?''

He snorted, and stopped polishing. ''What do you want from me? You know damn well I'm being blackmailed into doing this. Do I have to like the woman, too?''

''Don't you?''

''I said she was okay.''

''Fine.'' Brenda folded her arms across her chest in that sulky way he knew all too well. ''Have you gone to see Mom lately?''

Oh, brother. Now she was on the offensive. ''Nope, and the subject is not open for discussion.''

''Have you at least talked to her on the phone?''

''Yeah, but I bet you already know that.''

''Mom might have mentioned you phoned her *last month.*''

He gave her an amused look and kept working.

''Nick, you can't blame her for wanting to see you

married and settled down with children before she dies.''

He stared at his sister in disbelief. ''For God's sake, she's only fifty-two. I doubt she has one foot in the grave already.''

''Yeah, but you know Mom.''

''Yeah, I do. That's why I'm staying clear until she either gets over this phase or starts picking on you instead.'' He stopped, and used the back of his hand to wipe his forehead. ''Why isn't she bugging you to get married and have kids?''

''Because I'm not the one turning thirty next year.''

''Ah, that explains everything.'' Shaking his head, he glanced skyward. The afternoon sun was fading. He had to get a move on. ''Look, if you want to keep yapping, grab a rag and help.''

''And ruin my manicure? I don't think so.''

''Too bad. If I don't finish, I just may have to cancel my appointment with Doc.''

''That is too bad.'' Brenda turned to go, and over her shoulder added, ''I hear Aspen is really nice in November.''

''You're a brat,'' he called after her.

''And proud of it. Don't keep Emma waiting.''

He watched her walk to her car, open the door and pause to waggle her fingers at him before getting in. After she'd driven away, he checked his watch again. No way was he going to finish in time for his date with Tiffany.

What the hell...Tiffany was a Porsche kind of gal anyway.

He finished the hood, threw the rag aside, and then stored all the cleaning supplies on the garage shelves he'd had the architect design when he had the house built last year.

The English Tudor was too big for one person, but on the advice of his accountant, he'd gone ahead and had it designed and built, but customized to suit his needs. Which meant he basically lived in the family room and the third garage where he kept the Chevy.

Unfortunately, his mother couldn't see the financial reason for such a big house, that he needed a sizeable mortgage to reduce his taxable income. All she wanted to see was that he was finally ready to give her grandchildren.

Like that would happen.

At least not anytime soon. There were too many Tiffanys in the world...lovely, willing and able, and wanting nothing more from him than a good time and an occasional trinket. He was of the opinion that you didn't fix what wasn't broken. He was extremely successful at dating. Marriage he might not be so good at. It was a risk he wasn't willing to take. Too many unknowns set you up for failure.

He checked his watch again. Time to move it. The sooner he got this ridiculous study over with, the better.

SHE WAS ALREADY IN THE LAB when he arrived, sitting at her desk, head bowed, feverishly scribbling notes. When she heard the door, she looked up and automatically pushed up those ugly, oversized, black glasses. And then she smiled.

Nick had to drag his gaze away from her mouth. Those lips were lethal. "I thought I might be too early again."

"This is my volunteer day. I'm off by four." She got up and came around the desk. Same style of baggy pants and shirt, only the colors were different. "What can I get you before we get started?"

"I guess a beer is out of the question."

"Definitely." She gave him a bland look. "Same choices as yesterday."

"Water's okay."

"Have a seat. I'll be right back."

"Don't hurry, Doc. I'm not going anywhere." Unfortunately for him that was true. He shrugged out of his jacket and tossed it over the back of the guest chair.

At the corner of the desk was a silver-framed picture and he went around to get a look at it. The photo was of an older couple standing in front of a church, her parents probably, although she didn't look anything like them. Other than that, there was nothing else personal on the desk, or the shelves or the walls. Everything seemed sterile in a cluttered sort of way. Given the amount of time he knew she spent here that surprised him.

"Here you go." She returned in less than a minute, an Evian for him and one for her. "The recorder is set. We can start as soon as you're ready."

"I'm ready." He unscrewed the top of his water, passed it to her, and then took hers and opened it for himself.

She seemed taken aback. "Uh, thank you."

"No problem." He took a swig, and then stared as she did the same.

Except when she tipped her head back and drank, it wasn't the mere act of swallowing. With her, it was an art form. Her entire face seemed to transform as she performed the simple task, turning it into an erotic pleasure. Her eyes had drifted closed and there was a slight flush to her skin. The way her full pink lips pursed around the opening, sucking in the water, gave him such a rush he immediately sat down, and hoped she hadn't noticed his growing interest.

It was crazy. This was Doc, someone in whom he had no sexual interest. Dammit, seeing the woman in the thong two days ago had gotten his motor revved. Brenda would probably call it something like transference. This reaction wasn't really about Doc. She was just another one of his sister's friends, career-driven, no passion unless it involved her work. Brenda hung out with those types of people. They all bored him silly.

Even physically Doc wasn't his type. The way she dressed showed her inhibition. And the way she blushed when he described his dreams. Okay, that was kind of cute. But their relationship was strictly professional.

Too bad his body didn't get it.

Maybe out of self-defense he'd have to ask about the mystery woman. Seeing her unexpectedly like that was the root of his problem—kind of like a fresh-baked apple pie you can smell and see, but you can't touch until after dinner. Of course then all you want is that damn pie.

He shifted to accommodate the snugness of his pants, and took another gulp of cold water.

She'd sat behind her desk again, and was checking the recorder, totally oblivious to his plight. When she picked up the bottle of Evian again, he nearly dove under her desk for cover.

This time she took only a quick sip, and then set the bottle aside and spoke into the recorder. "Wednesday, day 2, subject—Nick Ryder."

The reminder was better than a cold shower. He was her subject, like a bug under a microscope. That's all.

She smiled at him. "How many dreams do you remember from last night?"

"Two."

"Excellent." Her finger poised over the record button. "Ready?"

"Sure." He pulled his folded notes out of his jacket pocket, aware that his mood had taken a sour turn.

"Do you have a title for this one?" As she started the recorder, there was a teasing twinkle in her eye that surprised him.

"Afternoon Delight."

She blinked, the twinkle was gone and she stared warily at him. "Go ahead."

Hell, she'd asked, hadn't she? He could have been more pithy and called it *Afternoon Quickie.* He cleared his throat, and glanced down at his notes. Not that he needed them. The dream had been another one of those romps that seemed so real that the aftereffects had lingered throughout the day.

"I'd just gotten out of a board meeting and decided to run home for lunch and to get my gym bag. Except it really wasn't my house. At first everything seemed okay to me until I got to the bedroom and tried to find the closet, and then I realized nothing looked familiar.''

"Did it look like your house in the beginning, or did you just have the sense that it was your place?''

"It looked nothing like my real house, but for whatever reason, I was okay with it. I believed that was my place until, like I said, the bedroom. It was huge and every time I thought I'd found a closet, I'd end up in some cavernous room." He paused, trying to wade through the foggy part of his memory.

"How were you feeling at that point?''

"What do you mean?''

"Anxious, curious, afraid?''

He frowned. "Confused and frustrated. Yeah, I wanted to get my gym bag so I could work out before my next appointment and I was frustrated that I wouldn't find it in time.''

She scribbled a couple of words down in her notebook, and then looked up expectantly.

Nick rotated a shoulder, trying to release the tension retelling the dream had surprisingly caused. "I finally figured I knew where the bag was but when I went into the next closet, it was semidark and the racks were empty. That's when I started to panic. I realized I was in the wrong house but I didn't know how to get out. I retraced my steps down the hall, but it was different this time...longer, darker and none of the doors along the way would open.

"A couple of times I thought I heard a cat, but when I stopped to listen, there was nothing. Just an eerie silence that made me want to get the hell out of there.''

"Again, how were you feeling?'' she asked, and

when he didn't immediately respond she added, "Panicked and fearful, perhaps?"

"Pissed. Helpless. I even punched a wall and pain exploded in my hand. I couldn't make a fist. I thought I'd broken it. And then I heard the cat again and forgot all about the pain."

When he lowered his voice, Emma rested her elbows on the desk and leaned a little closer. She doubted he even realized he'd dropped to a whisper. He was really getting into the retelling. Feelings of fear and desperation prompted by the dream were resurfacing and played across his face with intriguing intensity.

Fascinating stuff. Certainly better than yesterday's interview. She'd begun to wonder if all he dreamt about was sex. If that had been the case, she didn't know how she was going to last two weeks. But this was great material. She had to force herself to listen only and not try to start analyzing the data. There'd be time enough for that later. Right now it was important they didn't lose momentum while he was comfortable enough to express himself.

The thought came too soon. She wasn't sure if it was her riveted expression that broke the spell, but he straightened suddenly, wariness etching tiny creases between his dark brows. He picked up the bottle of Evian and took a long slow sip. After he put it down, he didn't seem in any hurry to resume talking.

"You were saying you heard the cat again." Her gentle prompt was met with a reluctant nod. "And then?"

"I thought it was a cat. It turned out to be a woman."

"A woman?" Emma sighed softly. Why was she not surprised? He'd titled the dream *Afternoon Delight*. She couldn't claim he didn't warn her. "Did you know her?"

"Nope. I could barely see her."

"Fill in the details from the second time you thought you heard a cat."

He slouched in his seat, pushed a restless hand through his hair. Embarrassment wasn't causing his reluctance. She was fairly certain of that after yesterday's no-holds-barred interview. She guessed his reticence had more to do with the way he'd let his guard down.

"Come on." She smiled. "You're doing great."

His gaze went to her mouth, and lingered for several eternal seconds. And then dread slowly washed over his face.

"What's happening? Did you just remember something?"

"I think so."

"Tell me before you lose it."

"I doubt I'll lose this one, Doc." He exhaled sharply. "I think the woman might have been the same one from the other dream."

Emma relaxed, disappointed it wasn't a breakthrough memory. "That's not uncommon, especially if she represents a particular person or conflict in your life."

His expression immediately shut down. The reference to a personal conflict probably did it.

"Let's go on," she said quickly. "What happened next?"

He stretched his neck in an obvious attempt to try and relax. "I saw her through the semidarkness. I could barely make out her form, but I could tell she was calling me, waving me toward her. Something told me it was all right to trust her and I moved forward, but she kept backing away. I started to get angry and frustrated again, but then she slipped into a room at the end of the hall.

"I followed her inside, but couldn't see her at first. Candles were lit everywhere. There must have been a hundred of them, the flames flickering like crazy and casting all kinds of shadows on the wall."

He paused, and she asked, "Was the room familiar to you in any way?"

He snorted. "It was like something out of a medieval novel. There was a big stone fireplace, the walls were made of stone, and the bed was massive with four ornately carved posters. The woman was lying in the middle of it on some bulky handmade quilts. She kind of blended in so she was hard to find."

"What was your first thought or feeling when you saw her?"

"Relief."

"And then?"

A slow smile curved his lips as his eyes met hers. "She was naked, Doc, not a stitch on her creamy smooth skin. You do the math."

5

OH, BROTHER. Emma tried to maintain a blank expression. It wasn't easy. "So it's fair to say you got a little excited."

"A little." His grin broadened.

"And then?"

"She waved me toward her, and call me crazy, but I ran for the bed."

"Could we skip the editorial, please?"

"But, Doc, you're always asking me to editorialize."

"You know what I mean." She took a calming breath. "Go on."

"I sat at the edge of the bed and just stared at her. She was so beautiful, with her long dark hair spread out over the cream satin pillow, her perfectly curved body, and her breasts—I couldn't look away. They were so—not just perfect but—I don't know." He shook his head, staring off somewhere out the window, looking genuinely bewildered. "The areolas were so big and pink and her nipples were like cherries. I absolutely couldn't drag my gaze away from them."

He glanced at her suddenly without a trace of self-consciousness. "You see, Doc, I'm normally a leg and butt man. Don't get me wrong, I like breasts, too, but this was a fascination I can't begin to describe.''

She briefly wondered if she should tell him what she thought this all meant. He wouldn't like it. She scribbled a note to herself, and then looked up for him to continue.

His gaze had lowered to her chest, and though there was no way he could see a thing through two layers of thick cotton, her breath caught in her throat and her nipples immediately tightened.

She swallowed hard and grabbed for her water. The open bottle flew across her desk. Nick jumped up at the same time she did, and in a tangle of arms, they both managed to catch the bottle before it hit the floor.

Nick's face was close, his breath warm on her neck. He had a hold of the bottom of the bottle, while she gripped the top.

"Okay, now what?"

"Let go. I've got it."

His elbow brushed her hardened nipple as he released his hold, and it slid from her hand, bounced against the side of the desk, spraying them both.

To her annoyance, Emma automatically muttered a curse.

Nick chuckled as he swiped at the moisture on his chin. "Now, Doc, how am I ever going to trust you again?"

"Sorry, it slipped."

"I figured that much out." He raised a hand and she flinched. "Easy." With the pad of his thumb, he wiped the dampness off her cheek. And then he studied her with a probing stare that set her nerves on edge.

"Let's get back to work."

"Emma?"

At the use of her name, she froze. "You have another drop here." He touched her face again, a touch so gentle she held her breath in anticipation, a helpless captive of his gaze. "And here," he said, dragging his thumb across her cheek, his dark eyes boring into hers.

She wasn't sure she could lift her leaden feet, but she forced herself to move back before she gave in to the sudden craving to have him rake his hands over her body. "Thank you."

She cleared her throat as she hurried around to her side of the desk. By the time she sat down, he still hadn't moved. He simply stared at her in mute concern.

"Nick? Do you need to take a short break?"

"Huh?" He seemed to snap out of his trance. "No, I'd rather get a move on, Doc. I have a date tonight."

"Fine." To her dismay she realized she hadn't stopped the recorder. Screw it. She had no desire to hunt for the point at which they'd left off. Besides, God forbid she should make Nick late for his date. "Go ahead."

He settled back into his chair, damp patches of T-shirt clinging to his chest, molding sinew and muscle, and distracting her. She forced her attention on her notes, pathetic as they were.

"Okay," he said, "her breasts were what I was describing, right?" She nodded, and reluctance again crossed his face. "This next part is kind of weird."

Great. She gave him an encouraging smile.

"The woman didn't say anything but I could tell what she wanted. She kept smiling and then cupped one of her breasts and lifted it up to me. I lowered my head and took her nipple into my mouth. It was so big and round and ripe I thought I'd embarrass myself right there. I tried not to suck on it too hard, but I couldn't get enough, and she kept pressing herself against my mouth and I kept sucking and sucking until I drew milk.

"I got embarrassed and pulled away, but she didn't seem to mind. She guided me to her other breast. It was like I was helpless to do anything but start sucking again, like I had no self-control at all." He paused again. "Weird, huh?"

He'd surprised her with the question and she wasn't sure she'd find her voice. She was humiliated to realize how turned on she was, how much she wanted his mouth on her nipples. "Most dreams are. Did you wake up then?"

He shook his head. "She unbuttoned my shirt and started rubbing her palms over my chest, going lower and lower until she unbuckled my belt and unzipped my pants. I was so turned on I tried to help her so we could get on with business, but she wouldn't let me. I started getting frustrated, and that's when I woke up."

She breathed a relieved sigh. "Do you always dream about sex?"

"Well, after that I had this dream about a small pretty white dog—"

"A dog? Oh, God." She nearly flew out of her chair.

"Not that kind of dream." His eyes filled with outrage. "Christ, what kind of pervert do you think I am?" He swore softly. "It was a perfectly normal dream about a lost dog."

"Oh, sorry."

He snorted. "Look who has sex on the brain."

Emma wisely reserved comment.

"I'm a twenty-nine-year-old, healthy, red-blooded male. Of course I dream about sex. But only about fifty percent of the time." His gaze narrowed. "That's about normal, right?"

"I suppose."

"You should know. You're the expert."

At his curt tone, she sighed. "I've obviously upset you, and I apologize. I wasn't judging, only commenting."

"I'm not upset, Doc. Just anxious to get this over with. I have a date tonight."

"So you said." She took off her glasses and rubbed the weariness from her eyes. "After you woke up, did you have trouble getting back to sleep?"

He peered at her, a slight frown drawing his brows together.

"What?"

"You have pretty eyes."

She shoved her glasses back on. "Thank you. About the dream, did you have any particular—what now?"

"Do you consider them green or hazel?"

"Impatient. I thought you wanted to hurry up and get out of here."

He grinned, and Emma wondered how many women he'd seduced with that smile. His lips were full, not too full so as to appear feminine, but enough to draw curiosity, and his teeth were perfectly straight and enviably white. He could sell a million tubes of toothpaste with one flash of that smile.

"You should wear contacts or smaller glasses. Those hide your eyes."

She let out a sound of exasperation. "Is fashion consulting another one of your hobbies?"

"One of my hobbies?" His confused expression quickly turned to understanding. "Ah, Brenda has been disparaging me and my sidelines."

"No, she hasn't. She said you had a lot of hobbies, that's all."

Pursing his lips, he nodded without conviction.

"She did," Emma argued. "It came up when I asked if you had time for the study, which could take another month if we don't get back to it."

He glanced at his watch. "Are we done with this dream? Shall we start the one about the dog?"

Was she ever tempted to wrap this one up. If she said she wasn't embarrassed she'd be a liar. This morning she'd even applied two layers of self-tanning lotion just so her face wouldn't be so obviously pink when it heated up. That's probably why he thought her eyes looked green.

She took a deep, fortifying breath. "I still have a few questions."

"Shoot."

She smiled. Tempting idea. "How did you feel once you were with the woman in bed?" He opened his mouth to respond and she quickly added, "I don't mean sexually."

Amusement lit his eyes. "I know what you meant,

Doc. Let's see...the panic had disappeared and I guess I felt at ease. No, it was more than that...kind of...I can't explain it.''

"Try. It's important.''

The wariness was back in his face. "This is where you analyze me, right? Suggest that the woman is really my mother.''

Emma laughed. "I doubt she's your mother.''

He slumped in his seat again. "That's reassuring.'' He shot her a suspicious look. "How much did Brenda tell you about our family?''

"Nothing much.'' She shrugged. "Regarding you, hardly anything at all. Of course she's mentioned you in the past, but as soon as we thought you might become a subject, I purposely avoided information about you so as not to color my perspective.''

"So, in your professional opinion, who do you think the mystery woman is?''

"I need to ask you more questions before I can reach a conclusion.''

"Chicken.''

She grunted. "Frankly, I'm surprised you want to know.''

"Yeah, me, too.'' He shrugged. "Just curious how you egghead types think.''

"Ah, so charmingly put.'' She gave him a patronizing smile. "You want an off-the-cuff opinion?''

"Sure.''

"All right.'' She glanced down at her notes, purely for effect. She knew exactly how to take that smug look off his face. "I think this woman represents your desire to change your life. Maybe you're reaching a point where you want to begin nesting, start a family—''

''Shit! I knew Brenda said something.''

''She did not. Brenda and I never discussed you or your family. I have no reason to lie.''

He stared at her with distrust. ''Why else would you come up with that load of crap?''

''Oh, please...this is remedial psychology. If you took only an introductory course in college you would have heard this theory.''

That gave him pause. ''Run it by me again.''

''You were probably looking at the woman as a mother figure all right, but not for yourself but as a candidate to bear your children.''

He stood. ''This is a waste of time. You've got it so wrong.''

''Maybe, but you asked.''

He paced to the window and stared outside. ''This is the part I hate, when you start poking and prodding inside my head. Does it ever occur to you guys that sometimes things are just as they appear?''

''Often, actually.''

''Maybe I was just horny last night. Ever think of that?''

''No, I can't say I gave it much thought.''

He turned slowly and glared at her. ''You think this is funny.''

''Not in the least.'' She was, however, fascinated at how disconcerted he'd become. As if she'd hit a nerve. The last thing she needed was to spook him. ''Look, you asked me to throw something out without studying the data and I grabbed the textbook explanation. It's not a big deal.''

"Yeah, okay, guess I'm just touchy about the subject." He exhaled loudly and rubbed the back of his neck. "My mother's been on my back lately about—never mind."

"I understand."

"Yours, too?"

At first she didn't get it. "Ah, no, I've been spared the 'it's time you settled down' speech."

"Wait. It'll come."

"My mother's much too self-absorbed to want grandchildren." Oh, God, she tried not to cringe. The words had fallen right out of her mouth.

His eyes narrowed slightly. "Not a bad thing, I guess."

She wasn't sure how to respond to that assessment so she merely shrugged. "Maybe not."

"Trust me on this. Most of my life I had all this freedom to make my own choices, and then all of a sudden I don't know what's good for me."

Emma smiled. He was trying to make her feel better. She saw the trace of sympathy in his eyes, not pity, thank God, but that kind of understanding that says "don't give your slip of the tongue a second thought." Her opinion of him climbed a notch.

"It's a mother thing, Nick. I wouldn't worry about it."

"I'm not worried. I just ignore her."

"Well, that's nice."

At her teasing sarcasm, one side of his mouth lifted. "Just until she gets past this phase and starts picking on Brenda."

Emma grinned, liking this side of him. She was also starting to get a better picture. Interestingly, as successful as Nick was in business and life in general, he seemed to have trouble with personal relationships. Shying away from his mother instead of confronting her, not wanting to give gifts face-to-face, girlfriend-hopping, all indicated a reluctance to get in too deep.

She thought back to her conversation with Brenda about how Nick had hung around with an older crowd. Maybe growing up too fast had forced him to skip some emotional development.

"How do you handle your mother?" he asked.

It took her a second to switch out of psychologist mode. "I moved."

He laughed. "And you have the nerve to badger me?"

"I wasn't badgering. Can we get back to the dreaming?"

His entire expression changed, his eyes suddenly full of misgiving, like he wanted to be anyplace but here. That quickly, their easy rapport was gone.

"Please don't bail out on me." Oh, God. She sounded pathetic and pleading, and woefully unprofessional.

She swallowed, and waited for his guarded expression to give something away.

"I didn't say I was backing out on you, Doc." His eyes remained noncommittal but his voice had lowered to a soothing timbre. "I said I'd do this study, and I'll honor that." Hope flashed in his face. "Unless you've decided I'm not an appropriate subject. If you have someone else in mind, or maybe you'd rather—" He stopped when she began shaking her head. "It was just a thought."

Was she fooling herself that Nick's phase of her

study would be accurate? Was she that desperate? He obviously didn't want to participate. On the other hand, he was being brutally honest about his dreams, which was what counted.

"I tell you what," she said after a moment's thought. "What if we don't discuss any more of my theories or conclusions?"

"You mean I just spill my dreams and then I'm outta here?"

"Of course I'll have to ask you some questions, just as I've been doing."

"No sweat. That part's easy enough."

Emma breathed deeply. "We'll wait until the end of the study before I dig any deeper."

He leaned forward, his eyes glittering in warning. "You and Brenda both assured me this had nothing to do with psychoanalysis."

"Right. I'm only interested in interpreting your dreams."

"You're splitting hairs, Doc."

"You don't believe in all this *nonsense* anyway. Why should you care about what opinions or conclusions I form?"

He met her challenge with a faint smile. "Touché."

She sighed. This was all her fault. She'd been so flustered during their first meeting that she hadn't set the groundwork properly. "This won't be difficult. I promise. I'll ask you a few questions about what's going on in your life so that I can try and relate your dreams. What you tell me will be up to you."

She couldn't believe she was willing to stoop so low in order to complete her thesis. She'd practically told him it was all right to hold back information, which of course, would compromise her study. What was even lower was that she'd be willing to use Brenda to fill in the blanks.

"Don't look so upset, Doc. Nothing's changed. Let's get started on the next dream. I think it'll make you feel a little better."

Why had she ever thought he had a nice smile? She gritted her teeth, started the recorder and picked up her pencil. "Whenever you're ready."

Nick shifted until he was relatively comfortable in the uncomfortable chair, and then folded his hands. "There were these twins, blond, tall. I think they were from Sweden."

At her look of disgusted disbelief he couldn't keep a straight face any longer. "Don't have a stroke, Doc. I'm kidding."

She rolled her eyes, and then gave him a "grow up" look.

She couldn't have done a better Brenda imitation if she'd tried. He swore the two must have practiced together.

"You want to hurry and wrap this session up, or you want to waste time joking around?" She stared at him over her glasses, looking very much like a schoolteacher, looking very unlike his brand of woman.

Still, he knew he should lay off teasing her. Generally she was able to hide her feelings and slip behind that stoic, professional mask, but not before he got a glimpse of the embarrassment and frustration that tinted her cheeks a pretty pink.

His intention wasn't to cause her discomfort. He

guessed he'd been looking for a way to distract her, steer her away from digging into him. It didn't take a master's in psychology to figure out that one. What he couldn't figure out was why he'd gotten so edgy about the whole analysis thing. She was absolutely right. He did consider this all nonsense so why give a damn about any pseudo discovery about his subconscious?

"Okay, I'll be straight. No twins, in fact, there's not a woman in this dream." At her raised brows, he added, "And I have never, nor will I ever bat for the other team."

Her wrinkled nose gave her a cute, confused look.

"I am one-hundred-and-ten-percent heterosexual."

"Ah." The ghost of a smile that played about her mouth gave her away. She knew damn well what he'd meant. "Start from the beginning, and tell me everything about setting, sensations..."

"I know the drill, Doc, but I'll warn you, this was a short one."

"That's fine." She pushed up her glasses and he decided he was starting to like the way she did that. "They don't all have to be marathons."

"Okay, I just didn't want you to think I was holding out on you."

"Why would I ever have such a ridiculous thought?" Wide-eyed, the picture of innocence, she didn't crack a hint of a smile.

He didn't bother to hide his grin. "In this one I was with my dog at a park, although I didn't recognize it."

She held up a silencing finger. Her nails were unpolished but they were neatly filed with a slight sheen to them. Sensible, just like the woman herself. "This dog, is it yours? I mean do you really have a dog?"

"Yup. Jackson Brown. He's a mutt, part Golden Retriever and part Lab. He was the one in the dream, and not metaphorically either. It was Jackson, all right."

She smiled, it seemed with approval, and an irrational wave of pleasure washed over him.

"We were playing Frisbee which we often do, but this time Jackson wouldn't bring back the damn thing. I'd throw it, and he'd catch it, and then run in the opposite direction. I'd yell at him that he wasn't playing the game right, and then I'd have to run after him."

He paused, trying to remember how he got the Frisbee back. "I don't know how I caught up with him or what happened, but I'd suddenly have the Frisbee, and I'd throw it and he'd catch it, and we'd go through the whole thing again."

"You sound frustrated even now. How did you feel at the time?"

He laughed. "Frustrated. I was pissed, too, and I felt a little scared, which didn't make sense. There was no threat." He watched her scribble a note. "But I'm sure you'll make something of that, Doc."

She ignored the taunt. "Were there any other people around?"

"Nope. Just Jackson and me."

"What else?"

He shrugged. "That was basically it."

"When Jackson ran with the Frisbee, where did he go?"

"In the opposite direction."

She briefly closed her eyes and massaged her right temple looking tired suddenly. "Okay, but did he run into a thicket of trees or out in the open?"

"Behind some trees. I couldn't even see him. I just ran into the trees, and then I suddenly had the Frisbee again."

She scribbled something, and when the phone rang, she muttered, "Excuse me," and absently reached for it as she finished her notes.

"Emma Snow."

As she listened to the caller, he watched her expression change from indifference to concern in two seconds flat.

"When?" she asked the caller, the anxiety growing in her eyes. She glanced at her watch. "I can be there in twenty minutes."

She hung up the phone and met his gaze, an apology already forming in her eyes. "I'm really sorry but I need to cut our session short."

"No problem." He hesitated, hoping she'd elaborate, amazed he cared about what troubled her. He should be damn glad he was getting off the hook early today, period.

She stood, and started unbuttoning her blouse.

Stunned, it took him a second to process what he could see with his own eyes. She looked so blasé, he wondered if *she* knew what she was doing.

"For the most part, we've covered everything we need to," she said, continuing to unbutton as she moved around the desk. "Leave your notes. That'll be helpful."

He'd tried to avert his gaze, but finally he had to look...

She had on a white T-shirt beneath the baggy cotton shirt.

Relief and disappointment kept him in his chair. Her round perfect breasts jutting out as she shrugged out of the top shirt kept his gaze glued to her.

"Can we meet at about two-thirty tomorrow?" she asked, otherwise paying him no attention as she dug in a lower desk drawer and pulled out her purse.

"Uh, sure," he finally answered when she looked curiously at him. "Is there anything I can help you with?"

She eyed him in measuring silence. "No, but thanks."

He shouldn't have felt slighted, but he did. The way she'd looked at him had done it, as if she'd thought about accepting his offer but decided he wasn't up to the task.

"The thing is, Doc, if you're going to ditch me, I think I deserve an explanation why."

Impatience flashed in her eyes. "I volunteer at an animal shelter. One of the dogs we recently took in has gotten out. He's not particularly friendly..." Her expression told him that was an understatement. "And I seem to be the only one he responds to. I don't want him or anyone else getting hurt."

"I see." Nick got up. "Guess you don't need me then."

She shook her head and smiled. "But thanks for asking."

Just as well she'd turned him down. He didn't want to keep Tiffany waiting.

6

NICK AWOKE IN A COLD SWEAT. He'd been having a dream—no, a nightmare, but he couldn't quite recall what it was about. Maybe it was best left buried in his subconscious, he thought, as he stared up at the ceiling. He'd never had this reaction before and he sure as hell didn't want Emma analyzing the hell out of it.

Emma.

Dammit. She'd been in the dream. But he wouldn't go there. What he couldn't remember wouldn't hurt him.

Even with the blinds shut he could tell the sun hadn't risen yet. He rolled over to see the digital alarm clock. Five thirty-seven. With a groan, he rolled back over and buried his face in the pillow. No one should be awake at this ungodly hour.

Ten minutes later, he sat up. It wasn't going to happen. Nick Ryder, who could usually fall asleep in a hot second, was as wide awake as a rooster. He peered through the semidarkness at Jackson lying beside him. The mutt's eyes were shut tight and not even a muscle twitched.

Nick grunted as he swung his legs to the floor. Any other morning Jackson would be whining in Nick's face to be let outside. Nick slid him another look.

Payback was tempting. He sighed, deciding to let the poor slob sleep.

Purposely trying to not think about the dream, or Emma, he showered and brushed his teeth. He skipped shaving. That would be overdoing it this early in the morning. When he got to the kitchen, he cursed, remembering that his coffee timer wasn't set to start brewing for another two hours. He manually started a pot, and then went in search of the newspaper, assuming that someone was foolish enough to get up this early to deliver it.

He found the paper in its usual spot in the middle of the driveway, and then headed for the spare garage where he kept the Chevy. The air was chilly and he wished he'd worn a jacket over his T-shirt, but then again he didn't plan on staying out long.

He just wanted to check the left front tire to see if it was still leaking air.

He'd just raised the garage door when he heard a car pull into the drive behind him. Had to be someone turning around. He glanced over his shoulder. It was Marshall's green Lexus that came to a stop a few feet away.

His friend got out already dressed in his conservative, gray, financial planner's suit and maroon tie. He had a large envelope in his hand.

Nick reared back his head. "What the hell are you doing up so early?"

"I was about to ask you the same thing."

"Are you on your way to work?"

Marshall nodded, but something seemed odd in his expression. It wasn't just that he looked tired. Who wouldn't be at this hour? He seemed tentative.

"Isn't this route out of your way?"

"Not really." Marshall shrugged. "I come this way sometimes."

"I think the coffee is done if you're interested."

"Sounds good. Here." He handed Nick the envelope as they went inside. "I was going to have this sent to you by courier today, but since I'm here..."

"My financial statement?"

Marshall nodded. "Quite impressive this quarter."

"Hell, I've been impressed the entire year." Nick tossed the envelope on top of the paper he'd left on the counter. "You've done a good job for me. I hope you've done as well for yourself."

His friend shrugged. "We're okay."

Nick led the way into the house, feeling uneasy about Marshall's response. Although Nick didn't want to pry, he knew Sally had quit her lucrative job two months ago in preparation for the birth of their third child. Having a heavy-duty mortgage and two kids couldn't be easy.

"You didn't tell me why you're up roaming around so early." Marshall took two mugs out of the cabinet. "Didn't you have a date with Taffy?"

"Tiffany. And yes, I met her for dinner."

His friend chuckled. "I take it you didn't get lucky."

Normally that question wouldn't have irked Nick. Why it did now he had no clue. "I was tired, so we called it an early night."

Marshall frowned. "Am I thinking of the right girl? She has really light blond hair to her shoulders and big casabas."

"That's her."

"You passed that up?" Marshall dumped so much cream and sugar into his coffee it made Nick's stomach roll. "You sick or something?"

"I will be if you put one more spoonful in there."

Marshall stared down at the tan-colored brew, his face creased in dismay. Obviously he hadn't realized what he'd done.

Nick took his first blissful sip. Strong and black, just the way he liked it. "How are Sally and the kids?"

"Driving me crazy."

Nick laughed.

Marshall didn't. "I don't know, Nick, I think you've got the right idea. Stay single."

"That's a load of crap. You don't mean that."

His friend smiled, and shrugged. "Sally wants to know when you can come to dinner."

"For her cooking? Anytime." Nick frowned suddenly. "She can't be in any shape to want to cook. Tell her I'll take everyone out. She can pick the place."

"You know her. She'll want to cook for you."

"Yeah, I know." He smiled. "She's an absolute doll. But I insist."

"I'll pass the offer along."

Nick's smile faded at Marshall's indifference. The guy was crazy about his wife and kids. What the hell was going on? "You sure you didn't stop by to talk or something?"

Marshall laughed now. "Like I thought you'd be awake. I really was just passing by." He looked at his watch and set down his mug. "I gotta get to the office."

Something was wrong. Nick was getting too many bad vibes, or maybe his vibes didn't work this early in the morning. "Hey, buddy, you know if you ever need to talk..."

His voice trailed off. He sucked at this kind of thing. Touchy-feely stuff wasn't his style. Fortunately, Marshall caught his drift and nodded. In fact, he looked as though he was about to say something, then thought better of it and clammed up.

Nick took a deep breath as he walked him to the door. "Stop by anytime, okay?"

Their gazes met, and Marshall's mouth curved slightly. "Thanks, Nick. I'll call you later this week about the game Monday night."

The game? Damn, he'd forgotten about the football game they'd agreed to go to. "Good. I'm looking forward to it."

He watched until Marshall backed all the way out of the drive, and still couldn't pinpoint what specifically about his friend's behavior was eating at Nick. Noticing he'd left the garage door open, he wandered in that direction, racking his brain for a missed clue.

Maybe he was the one all jumbled up. After last night, it was a miracle he could think straight at all. Another fragment of the dream drifted into his thoughts and his heart pounded like a damn jackhammer. Good thing he didn't have anything important to do today. No way would he be able to concentrate.

He saw a smudge on the Chevy's fender and grabbed a rag. Unfortunately, he did have one appointment this afternoon...

The thought of having to see Doc made him sweat. More dream fragments flooded his head. Right now he'd give just about anything to get out of the study. Maybe even kiss off Aspen.

Oh, hell.

He nearly collided with a couple of stacked boxes he'd meant to go through a week ago. He couldn't remember what he'd stored in them and would probably end up getting rid of the contents but he wanted a look inside first. He started to step around them, and then realized this was the perfect project to distract him.

After attacking the smudge with vigor, he threw aside the rag, and opened the top box. Two trophies, one he'd received in high school for baseball, and the other for college tennis, sat on the top of some old magazines. He smiled at the memory of the embarrassing time his mother had gone camera-happy. Getting the baseball trophy hadn't been that big a deal, but she'd taken three rolls of film at the presentation ceremony. The guys at school had teased him for a week.

He'd be exactly that kind of parent, he thought suddenly, and surprising the hell out of him. Making a big production of all the events in his kids' lives. He hadn't realized until this moment that that was where most of his confidence stemmed from.

As far as his mother had been concerned, he and Brenda could do anything. She never criticized, but celebrated their successes, and downplayed their failures, pointing out that no one excelled at every aspect of life. She'd refused to dwell on their shortcomings, or let them wallow in it, claiming that was energy ill spent.

A warm burst of pride and gratitude filled his chest.

Funny how your parents seemed to get smarter as you got older.

He'd tell her that the next time he saw her, thank her for giving him such a healthy approach to life.

Unless she started in on the home, hearth and family bit again. He shuddered at the thought. The lady made Attila the Hun look like a nursemaid when she got on her high horse about his future, or lack thereof.

He set aside the trophies, and laughed out loud when he saw which magazines had been stacked beneath them. Picking up the first copy he'd ever bought of *Midnight Fantasy,* he leafed through the brittle pages. He'd been fifteen at the time, if he remembered correctly, and had to rotate hiding places so Brenda or his mother wouldn't find it.

He flipped to the centerfold and stared at the curvaceous blonde who'd given him a hard-on for a week. She looked different than he remembered. She was pretty, seductive, the whole nine yards…just different.

The next few pages were advertisements, and then he came to the reader letters. He'd completely forgotten about them, and how they'd kept him spellbound for hours. Amazing he'd ever thought they could be real experiences, but at fifteen, his hormones weren't all that rational.

The letters were actually stories describing bizarre sexual experiences, told more to tantalize than be accurate, each one more outrageous than the last. He scanned the first few, and had to admit they packed a wallop…even at his ripe old age.

Before he knew it, he sat down on his workbench and started reading in earnest. He started to remember a few of the stories with amazing clarity. Clearly they'd made an impression on his feeble fifteen-year-old mind. No wonder he'd had the kind of dreams he'd had for most of his adult life. All this surreal stuff had been like grist for the mill.

In spite of himself, he continued to read, one magazine after the other, and before long the morning was gone. He looked at his watch and swore. He had to meet Doc in two hours. The thought was like fingernails on a chalkboard. He couldn't tell her about last night's dream…

Memories rushed him like an avalanche before he could raise his defenses. The long-haired woman in his dream…last night…the other two nights…

Doc.

How could he have not known it was her? Denial? Possibly.

Shaken, he took a deep calming breath. It didn't help much. He'd learned something else startling last night, something he'd been too stupid to see. There was no mystery woman. There was only Emma.

What the hell was he going to do for their session? Describe in detail all the hot things he wanted to do to her? No way he'd tell her she'd taken center stage in his dreams.

His gaze went back to the issue of *Midnight Fantasy* sitting in front of him. But he could borrow someone else's fantasy.

Until he convinced Emma they should create a few of their own….

EMMA'S LIFE WAS going to hell in a handbasket. She finally understood the old country phrase. Her part-

time job was at the top of the list of factors under-
mining her sanity. She struggled out of her uniform,
and winced when she heard a rip. Great. Now she had
to get out the needle and thread. No big deal...it
wasn't as if she didn't have oodles of time on her
hands.

Groaning, she glared at the wall clock. Nick would
be here in five minutes. Unless he was early, which
was how her luck was running today. The thought put
more spring in her movements and she quickly pulled
on a pair of jeans. Not her preferred lab attire but it
was the only thing clean.

Three great reasons had prompted her to take the
waitress job at Darby's Bar and Grill. First, the tips
were excellent. Second, it wasn't a college hangout
so no one would recognize her. Third, the hours were
perfect without any pressure.

Right now, none of those reasons seemed worth-
while. The job had become more complicated. As
soon as her thesis was accepted and she could start
working full-time at the clinic, she'd throw herself a
huge resignation party. Nothing but wine coolers and
chocolate-dipped strawberries. And she'd eat herself
silly.

The thought cheered her a little as she pulled on
her white cotton lab shirt over a pink T-shirt. There
was a small tan spot on the breast pocket, probably a
leftover from the chicken sandwich she'd wolfed
down in the car yesterday. Nothing a little Wite-Out
wouldn't cure.

She left the back room just as Nick entered the lab.
He looked awful. Tired. Run-down. And then he
flashed that killer grin.

"Hey, Doc, what's shaking?"

"My thighs," she muttered to herself, vowing to lay off the French fries for a while. "Nothing much. I hope you had an active night. Dream-wise, anyway."

He looked nervous briefly, and then his grin widened. "Did you say your thighs?"

Emma groaned. He couldn't possibly have heard that. But obviously he had. She gave him an I-don't-know-what-you're-talking-about look.

"Tell you what, Doc. I'll let you off the hook. You can owe me one."

"Gee, how swell of you."

"Now there's a term I haven't heard in a while." He took his usual seat, and then swiveled around and simply stared at her. As though she might bite...

Or maybe as if he'd like to bite her.

The idea was like an electric shock. She quickly looked away. It was too late. The quiet intensity in his eyes had already stolen her breath. She turned toward a file cabinet for privacy as she gulped for air.

What the hell had just happened? It seemed as if everything changed between them in the space of a heartbeat.

All because of one look.

Ridiculous. She was tired, that's all.

She turned around and was relieved to see he wasn't paying any attention to her. His gaze was focused on the leather lounger in the corner. Good. Exhaustion she could handle.

"I've been meaning to ask you about that chair," he said. "Who gets to use it? Or is it reserved for your naps?"

"Don't I wish." She barely stifled a yawn in time as she sank into her own chair. Good thing it wasn't too comfortable or she'd probably nod off. "We'll be moving over there toward the end of next week and I assure you, it will be all yours."

Alarm darkened his eyes, and he sat up straighter. "What's happening over there?"

"At the end of the study, the last two days to be exact, I'll monitor you while you're sleeping, and hopefully, deep in REM. But I'll explain all that later. Ready to get started?"

"Whoa." This time his entire face darkened. "Why didn't you explain this phase before?"

"Didn't I?"

His murderous glare was answer enough.

The thing was, she really thought she'd covered that area, in fact had covered the entire study, but she'd been off-kilter that first day and it was very possible that...

"You don't need to keep looking at me like that. If I omitted anything, it certainly wasn't done on purpose." She sighed. "It'll only take a couple of hours each time."

"I don't like it."

"It's not a big deal."

He scowled at the chair. "Yeah, right."

She didn't know why the idea made him so uncomfortable but he was genuinely annoyed. And nervous again. Not good. Trying to ignore the warning bells in her head, she readied the recorder. She hadn't had a chance to set it up yet, and she was glad for the distraction. He kept silent for the next minute while she made her adjustments, and when she finally looked up she caught him studying his notes.

He hadn't done that before. Made her wonder how many dreams he had for her today. The excitement simmering in her belly was purely professional, she told herself. It had nothing to do with the anticipation of more of his tantalizing subconscious escapades. Nothing at all.

He looked up suddenly, as though he were aware of her interest.

"Ready?" she asked brightly.

"Ready." He didn't seem too enthusiastic.

She pressed record and picked up a pencil.

He noisily cleared his throat. "I'm not sure where this dream takes place. Someone's house, which I can describe, but I don't know the woman in the dream, or if it's her house."

"Okay, start where you feel comfortable." She had a funny feeling something was wrong. It wasn't like him to qualify the dream before he began, or volunteer information, yet she sensed a certain reluctance. "Just don't leave anything out."

"I won't, Doc. Count on it."

There. She felt it again. An inner warning that made the skin at the back of her neck prickle. "Good."

"All right, so I'd just come home from work and was about to get—"

"Sorry, but I need to interrupt. Is this the beginning?" she asked, and he nodded. "So it starts off at your house?"

"No. I don't know where we are." He exhaled sharply. "Let me start again. I had just finished work.

And no, I don't have a regular nine-to-five job but I do sit on a couple of boards and I often have to climb into a suit and attend meetings. Maybe I was coming back from one, I don't know, but I had on a suit and tie and carried a briefcase.

"A woman was waiting for me in a house I assume was hers because I didn't recognize it. She was tall, with long blond hair and she was wearing only a short silk kimono. She immediately took the briefcase from me, set it aside and handed me a glass of wine. And then she told me she had a surprise for me before dinner."

"Did you have a sense that perhaps you lived with this woman?" Emma asked when he paused for a breath. "That it was a daily routine to go to this house after work or for dinner?"

"No, I think she was just a..." He smiled. "Playmate."

Emma nodded. "Go on."

"She took me by the hand and led me down a hall into a bathroom where she'd filled this enormous tub with warm sudsy water that smelled faintly of vanilla. Beside it on the tiled ledge was an ice bucket holding a bottle of champagne and a single glass. She took my jacket, loosened my tie and pulled my shirttails out from the waist of my pants. Slowly she unzipped my fly and then cupped my crotch for a second.

"I got excited, thinking we'd have a quickie, but she stepped back, her hands falling to her sides, and said I was to soak in the tub until she came for me. I asked her to join me but she said she had other things to do. I pulled her toward me and pushed the kimono off her shoulder, exposing her breast, licked her nipple until it hardened and then took it in my mouth.

"She moaned a little and pushed herself deeper into my mouth, but then she suddenly backed up and shoved me away. She told me I had to be patient because there was so much more to come, and then she left. So I poured myself some champagne, got into the tub and relaxed until I started to doze. The next thing I knew she was standing over me, tugging at my hand, telling me it was time to get out.

"So I did, and she handed me a towel. I remember it smelled like roses, which was a real turn-on, but when I tried to kiss her she kept backing away saying it wasn't time yet. But then she took the towel from me and started rubbing it over my body. I was rock-hard by then but she ignored it and dried me off. But then she knelt down in front of me and drew the towel down my legs."

A soft purring sound coming from his jacket startled them both. He made a face, and then a quick grab. "Sorry," he muttered, "it's my cell phone. I'll only be a minute."

Emma nodded and stopped the recorder as he got up, answered the caller and paced toward the window. She couldn't have welcomed the interruption more. Inside she was a mess. It would probably be polite to go to the back room and give him some privacy, but the thought of moving overwhelmed her. All she could manage was to sink back in her chair like a boneless blob.

This guy's dreams were worthy of the Dream World Hall of Fame...if there were such a thing. His recollection of the detail was remarkable.

She blinked.

Too remarkable, she figured, now that she wasn't too hot and bothered to think about it. She swung a suspicious glance his way. He stared out the window as he listened intently to the caller. Of course Brenda had told her he was the perfect candidate for that reason. But still...

"Sorry about that." He turned off the phone, stuck it back in his jacket pocket and sat down. "No more interruptions."

"No problem," she murmured, and started the recorder.

"I left off with her drying me with the towel, right?"

Emma nodded, amazed at his lack of self-consciousness. He could've been discussing the weather.

"Okay, she was kneeling down, and..." He paused, shrugged, showing the first sign of being uneasy. "How else can I say it? I was poking right at her face and she kissed the head. Lightly, trying to tease me, and then she finished drying my legs.

"Of course I was ready to explode and when I tried to get her to take me in her mouth, she stood and told me to be patient again. I reached under her kimono to try and convince her otherwise, and she was so wet I thought I had her, but she wouldn't give in. She pushed me away and told me to wait for her on the hammock in the sunroom.

"I did as she asked, but I wasn't happy about it. It's weird because I knew exactly where the room was without her telling me. There were lots of glass windows and a bunch of plants, mostly tropical ferns. The hammock was strung up near a bay window overlooking the pool outside.

"She'd already put on an Eagles CD and placed another silver ice bucket with champagne in it alongside the hammock. It was getting dusky outside but only two candles were lit. Still naked, I climbed into the hammock, laid back, and closed my eyes, listening to 'Take It To the Limit.' I don't know how long I laid there before she came back, but when I opened my eyes I saw her standing in the shadows. I motioned for her to join me, and she untied the kimono and let it fall to the floor."

He stopped and frowned at her. "Is anything wrong?"

"Wrong?" She straightened, clutched her pencil as if it were a lifeline. "No. Why?"

"You look a little peaked."

"I didn't get much sleep last night," she murmured, tightening her slackened jaw, and hoping he didn't get the wrong idea about her reaction. Which, of course, would be the right idea. She just didn't want him to know how incredulous she was, and helplessly turned on.

"Join the club," he said, sounding totally unaffected.

"Excuse me?"

"You said you couldn't sleep last night. Me, neither."

She laughed. "When did you come up with all this?"

He looked startled. "What do you think woke me up?"

"So this is the end of it?" she asked, hopeful and disappointed at the same time.

His slow, sexy grin was her answer. "Ready to continue?"

"Ready." She glanced at the recorder. It was still going.

"Okay, so the kimono fell off." He frowned, as if trying to remember what came next.

Sure. He was probably reliving the whole thing.

"Okay, that's right, she was totally naked, all of her skin shaved smooth, and her breasts were enormous, much bigger than they'd looked before."

Of course. Emma sighed.

"Did you say something?"

She shook her head and pretended to write a notation.

He waited for her to look up again. "I told her to come join me in the hammock, but she wouldn't budge. She said there was something else she wanted me to do first." His gaze carefully held Emma's. "She told me to jerk off, and then she slipped her hand between her legs."

7

NICK WASN'T MISTAKEN. He saw the burning hunger in Emma's eyes. She was turned on. That hadn't been his intention. He'd thought she'd be embarrassed, maybe even ready to deem him an unsuitable subject and release him from the study. Instead, her reaction created a new problem. If she so much as crooked her little finger, he'd have her on her back in seconds flat.

It wasn't just the story making him harder than Mount Fuji, or even the memory of seeing her half naked, it was the way she kept moistening her lips, and breathing so hard her chest rose and fell in hypnotic rhythm. She'd be mortified if she knew her reaction was so obvious, but he doubted she was aware of any of it.

His gaze moved to her hands and the way she lightly scraped her nails across the notebook paper. He could almost feel them raking his back, encouraging him to go deeper.

He swallowed, and forced his thoughts away from the foolish web his mind recklessly wove. Nothing was going to happen between him and Doc. She wasn't the type who'd be satisfied with a dinner out now and again, and casual sex on the side. And he wouldn't be happy with anything more.

It was strictly business between them, and hopefully that wouldn't be for much longer.

His gaze drew to her glistening lips. Unless he could convince her a little casual sex never hurt anyone. "You know, Doc, I could really use a drink of water."

She blinked, and her hands stilled. "Me, too," she said, and abruptly stood.

He waited until she was out of the room to adjust the front of his jeans. They'd gotten unbearably tight, and no amount of rationale had dampened the eagerness beneath his fly. Man, was he a first-class idiot, or what? If this scheme to get out of the study backfired on him, it would serve him right.

"I'm afraid it's not—"

At the sound of her voice he shifted positions. But it was too late. She had to have seen him fixing his jeans.

"Um..." She noisily cleared her throat. "The water isn't very cold." She returned to her chair, and keeping her gaze averted, pushed a bottle of Evian across the desk at him. "I didn't put them in the refrigerator soon enough."

Her face grew steadily pinker as she opened her own bottle and guzzled half of it.

"No problem," he mumbled, and gulped down most of his. "Do you want to take a break, or anything?"

Her gaze flew up. "Is there much more?"

"Not really."

"Then let's go ahead and finish up." Her eyes narrowed. "Unless *you'd* like a break. That would be okay."

"No, I'm fine." Dammit. He didn't want them to be uncomfortable with each other. "I gotta ask...do you want me to continue with as much detail?"

She was torn. Indecision showed in her eyes, and the way she nervously shoved up her glasses made him sorry he even asked.

"Go ahead with as much detail as you're comfortable with describing. If you'd prefer, summarize and hopefully I'll get the picture."

Their eyes slowly met, and Nick stared for a moment, trying to figure out if he'd picked up the right signal. Was she interested? If she wasn't, she was a damn tease.

Or maybe naive? No, he didn't think so. Which meant all bets were off now. He was going for it. If she wasn't interested in a harmless fling, she had to tell him.

At the thought, adrenaline surged and he had to concentrate to get back into the dream. "Let's see...I believe I left off with her telling me to, let's say, please myself. I begged her to come and participate and she reminded me I needed to be patient. In the meantime, she was doing a good job of getting herself off, and I couldn't stand it a second longer and I started to do as she'd asked.

"I stroked myself slowly at first so it wouldn't all be over too soon. But she was really getting into it, rubbing her hands all over her breasts and belly, between her legs, moaning until I couldn't stand it. I was about to come but she rushed over and stilled my hand, and told me it wasn't time. And then she ordered me to turn over.

"I wrapped an arm around her waist and tried

coaxing her in beside me by sucking her nipples, kissing and licking the skin between her breasts. When I tried to put my finger in her, she stepped back and demanded I turn over.''

Nick paused to take another sip of water. He wasn't thirsty but if he kept watching Emma's heated reaction, he was not going to be able to hold onto his restraint.

She grabbed her own bottle of Evian and took a big gulp. No, she wasn't about to dismiss him. He'd bet she was just as horny as he was. The idea was distracting, making him dwell on when he should make his move rather than on the pseudo dream.

Her expectant look reeled him in, and he set down the water and took a deep breath. ''I turned over as she asked, and since this was one of those woven, net type hammocks, you can pretty much guess what happened since I was already saluting the flag. I poked right through and just hung there. I saw her get to her knees before she ordered me to bury my face in the pillow, and I knew what was coming. Or at least had high hopes.''

He grinned.

Doc didn't look amused. In fact, she started to look irritated. What brought that on?

''The woman showed no mercy. She closed her mouth over me and sucked relentlessly, retreated briefly, and then started over again until I couldn't hold back any longer. But even after I came, she wouldn't let go. She tongued me, slow even strokes up and down my shaft until I was hard again. I thought I was going to explode, and I begged her to join me on the hammock. She stopped sucking, but let her tongue trail over the tip and then started a swirling motion.

"I couldn't stand it. I knew I'd come again without pleasing her so I pushed off the hammock. I surprised her and I was able to catch her around the waist. We both sank to the floor and I parted her thighs, and found her wetness with my mouth. She struggled for a moment, but as soon as my tongue touched her she went limp. She grabbed my hair and pulled me closer, forcing my tongue to slide deeper inside.

"She sounded like she was about to come so I raised myself and thrust inside her. She was wet and slippery and I sank so deep she screamed. And then I felt her convulsing around me, her muscles gripping me until I came again."

He'd been staring off toward the window as he relayed the "dream," but his gaze slowly met Doc's. She looked somewhat stricken. He suddenly wasn't feeling so hot himself. Scratch that. He was hot, all right. Even his blood pressure rocketed out of control.

He took a hasty sip of water, wiped his mouth with the back of his hand, and realized he wasn't so steady. How the hell was he going to finish the rest of the story? He'd already done a ruthless job of editing the original version. "That's it. I woke up."

She didn't move, only stared at him with wary misgiving. A faint pink tinted her cheeks and she'd drawn her lower lip between her teeth. She put a hand to her flushed throat and loosened her collar. "This sounds an awful lot like fantasy."

He shrugged, hoping his pants would start to loosen. The only way he'd stand up right now is if someone yelled fire. "Most of my dreams are." Her abrupt frown had him adding, "I've always been pretty superficial in that department. Hell, Doc, how many men do you know who wouldn't want to find themselves in that situation?"

She gave him a bland look. "We obviously travel in different circles."

"Right." His short bark of laughter brought annoyance to her eyes. "Then you have some pretty strange male friends."

Or maybe she didn't have any. The thought nagged him. "Doc, do you have a boyfriend?"

"That is irrelevant, and none of your business."

"Yeah, I know. Do you?"

She made a sound of utter exasperation. "Can we finish this up?"

"Sure." He gave her a lazy smile that seemed to heighten her annoyance. "I assume you have questions."

She returned a measuring look before lowering her gaze to consult her notes. The thing was, the top page of her notebook was blank. He watched as it took a few seconds for her to realize she hadn't taken any notes, and when she finally met his eyes again, anger and humiliation sparked like the Fourth of July across her face.

He said not a word, but waited patiently for her to gather her wits. It didn't take her long to regroup. Amazing, the way she calmly checked the point of her pencil, and then lifted her chin and stared back at him.

"I want to do something a little different this time," she said coolly...so coolly it made him nervous. "We're going to diagram your dream."

He frowned. "How?"

"It's very simple. Tell me the dream again—" Her eyebrows shot up. "Not in detail. Summarize it, and we'll highlight the different elements of the dream."

"Huh?"

"Almost every element of a dream can be placed in one of six categories, which are: setting, people, feelings, objects, animals, and action or situation. If we break these down, it'll be easier for you to record your future dreams and to interpret them."

The hair on the back of Nick's neck reached for the ceiling. She was obviously back in control, the consummate professional. And she was up to something. Was this some sort of payback?

She met his intense, probing stare with a look of total innocence.

Or maybe she liked hearing him describe the sex. Maybe it made her so hot she wanted to replay the whole thing. Maybe he'd get lucky.

"I thought I was doing a pretty damn good job of recording my dreams already." He carefully watched her face, looking for clues, hoping she was ready to take the leap. His sheets were clean and ready. "How much more detail do you want?"

She flushed. "I'm trying to make things easier for you to keep focused on the structure of the dream and possibly enable you to recognize parallel situations or feelings in waking life."

"See, Doc, there you go." He shook his head. "Assuming I want to know what all this crap means. Which is absolutely nothing, in my opinion."

"Fine. Then do it for me, okay? It'll help make my job easier."

"How so?"

Her color deepened. "It's difficult to explain. Can we continue now, or were you planning on staying all night?"

"I don't know, Doc. What did you have in mind?"

She scrunched up her mouth in a cute, disapproving pout. She didn't say anything though. He figured she was thinking of a way to best him. And here he'd been a good sport in not pointing out that this diagramming crap was a shield, a reminder to her to be professional.

Finally, she gave him a slow, tolerant smile. "Why, Nick? What did *you* have in mind?"

He mentally applauded her spunk. "Well, Doc, are you sure you want to hear it?"

She moistened her lips, her tongue darting out in a nervous swipe that left her glistening wet. God, she was killing him. "If it pertains to your dreams."

He smiled. "I'll tell you what I think last night meant. I went to bed horny. I dreamt about great sex. You get the picture."

"Okay, now we're getting somewhere." She straightened, the interested gleam in her eye making him edgy. "You didn't know the woman, right?" He nodded. "So the sex was anonymous, just like in your other dreams."

Ah, shit! "I know where you're going with this, Doc. You're wrong."

She gave him one of those serene, tolerant smiles that got on his nerves. "Tell me."

"Yeah, right, like I'm gonna waltz right into your trap."

She reared her head back in genuine surprise. "Trap?"

"Don't give me that innocent look." He eyed her with distrust. She'd obviously been talking to Brenda. "You think I'm commitment phobic."

"I see we share the same conclusion." The tolerant smile broadened to one of satisfaction. "You're starting to get the hang of this."

He snorted, tempted to tell Her Smugness she was analyzing a fictitious story out of a magazine. "I like having a good time. I'm not ready to be tied down. That does not make me commitment phobic."

"Okay, so maybe phobic is too strong a word, but the fact that you never know who any of these women in your dreams are does suggest that— What?"

"Nothing." He shrugged a shoulder. "You look cute when you have that superior act going on."

"Hmm." She leaned back and stared thoughtfully at him, her brows slightly furrowed over the ugly black glasses.

"Hmm, what?"

"Nothing." She smiled, and then hunched over her notebook to scribble something.

He tried to see what she'd written but her arm blocked his view. He'd be damned if he'd ask, though. Why should he? That would indicate he gave a rip about her misguided conclusions.

"Let's get back to the diagramming." She stopped writing and leaned back. Whether intentional or not, her hand obstructed his ability to see her notes. "Of course I need your cooperation."

"Haven't I been cooperating?" He gave her a persuasive grin, the one that usually sucker-punched women, no matter what their mood.

Doc lifted one dubious brow. Her lips didn't so much as twitch. ''Here's what I'd like you to do— form a couple of summarizing sentences about the gist of your dream and then dissect it by breaking down the elements.''

He groaned. She was so damn serious all the time. ''For example?''

She leaned back and glanced at the ceiling as she thought. Even through the ugly glasses she had pretty eyes. Green and golden flecks kept them from being merely brown, and he'd noticed that the green deepened when she was annoyed with him.

''I have a suggestion, Doc. Summarize the dream I just gave you as an example.''

Her eyes widened slightly, and she shoved the glasses up the bridge of her nose. ''Okay,'' she said, slowly, evenly. ''Let's see...it would go something like this— After work one day, I met my girlfriend who'd been waiting for me with a special surprise. While she made us dinner, she had me soak in a candle-lit bath and then—'' she faltered, her throat working with a nervous swallow.

''We had hot sex,'' he finished for her.

''And then made love,'' she said at the same time.

He gave his head an emphatic shake. ''No, just sex.'' Their eyes met and locked. ''It's always just sex.''

She nodded, her gaze flickering away. ''Okay, good. That's the kind of specifics you need to look at when diagramming. Now, you'll need to rework that summation in your own words, and then flag each of the different elements." She brought her gaze back to his and frowned. "What now?"

"Huh?"

"Why are you looking at me like that? Wasn't that clear?"

He straightened, unaware he'd been staring. She was an odd one. Not like most women he knew. She wasn't totally immune to him, he knew that, or at least not to the sensuality of his dreams. Nor was she the bookworm type he'd first thought. Even as embarrassment pinkened her cheeks, she remained cool and professional.

A woman of mystery, after all—definitely a new experience for him, and not one that was particularly appealing. He liked classifications. It made life simpler. And that thought probably surprised him most of all.

"Nick, are you listening?"

"Yeah, I heard you."

"Well, then a response would be appropriate."

Shit! Maybe he hadn't heard her. "I'm thinking, okay?"

She gave him one of her tolerant smiles again, though this one tighter, verging on disapproval. "A simple yes or no answer would do."

"Fine. I admit it. I wasn't listening. I was wondering what you'd look like without those glasses and your hair down."

She stared blankly at him, not giving a single thought away. Finally, after several long seconds, she put down her pencil and clasped her hands together. "I'd hoped you'd take this seriously."

Looking down her nose at him, censure and disappointment puckering her brows, she looked like Mrs. Cheese, his high school principal. He'd had enough head-butting with her over his afternoon absenteeism. His excuse that he was bored witless hadn't endeared him to her. No matter that he'd never slipped from the honor roll.

"Tell me," he said with a deliberately studious frown, "as a psychologist, how would you interpret that tactic you took?"

That earned him a startled look. She tilted her head to the side, frowning back. "What tactic?"

"Avoidance of your own sexuality."

She blinked, a surprised laugh tumbling from her lips...lips that were proving an increasing distraction. "I'd love to hear how you came up with *that* one, but we still have a lot of work to do."

"Right." He gave her a patronizing smile.

She glared for a moment, but didn't go for the bait. "Are you ready to resume, or—" she paused, a touch of uncertainty in her eyes. "Have you grown tired of this, too?"

At first he didn't get it. Yeah, he bored easily, but why would... "Brenda."

Doc's gaze flickered away.

"I thought you said you hadn't discussed me with my sister," he said, not bothering to keep the irritation out of his voice.

"We didn't discuss you. Like I already told you, when she called to tell me you'd do the study, I was concerned you wouldn't be able to commit to the entire two weeks."

"Gee, I'm glad she had enough confidence in me to think my attention span could last that long."

"It wasn't like that."

This was stupid. He didn't know why it suddenly bothered him that everyone thought he was a slack-off. No, that wasn't accurate. He'd accomplished too much, made enough money to embody the American symbol of success. But he liked his life uncomplicated. He liked sticking to what he knew instead of risking failure. So what? He didn't have a wife and kids. His financial responsibilities were met promptly.

Doc cleared her throat, and he snapped out of his preoccupation. "Look," he said, "I don't care what my sister told you. I'm here, doing your study. That's all that should matter."

"But she didn't say anything, really. She merely mentioned something about you getting past your latest hobby of playing with old cars."

He grunted with disgust. "A '55 Chevy is hardly an old car. It's a classic, dammit."

"No way." Her eyes widened.

"What?"

"A '55 Chevy? Standard? Classic body?"

Stunned, he nodded. "Peach and gray two-tone Belair."

Color brightened her cheeks and her eyes danced with excitement. "A convertible?"

"Yep." Pride warmed him. They were talking about his baby. "White canvas Carson top, best custom top they ever made."

"You got that right." She shook her head. "This is unbelievable."

"How do you know all this?"

"A friend of mine had one."

"Here?"

"No, back in Utah. Mr. Salisbury was an elderly neighbor." Her expression turned slightly guarded. "We'd better get back to work."

"Did he have tuck and roll upholstery?" He really wanted to ask more about her life in Utah, but a personal question obviously wouldn't be welcome.

She nodded, grudgingly, but some of the interest was back in her face.

"Custom chrome wheels and Hurst linkage?" he asked, and was fascinated with the way her eyes glowed. Shit! Like this was foreplay. "I have the exact same one."

She tilted her head. "Are you putting me on?"

"Hell, no. I restored that baby myself." He shrugged, trying to tamp down the pride pumping through his veins. He'd almost walked away from the project, frustrated because for the first time in his life, solutions weren't handed to him on a silver platter. But he'd stuck it out and worked long and hard to achieve perfection. It ended up being one of his most gratifying accomplishments. "Maybe you could come by my place and see it sometime."

The guarded expression was back, pinching her features. "Maybe."

She might as well have said no. He knew damn well she had no intention of making an appearance at his house. So what was up with that? Did she think he had an ulterior motive?

Okay, maybe he did, but he really was proud of the Chevy.

"We still have a lot of work to do."

He blinked, and met her gaze. She wore that schoolmarm expression again, as if he were a way-

In His Wildest Dreams

ward child whose attention had wandered, but she gave him a faint smile.

He ignored it. She didn't want to associate with him? Fine. Plenty of women did. Like Tiffany.

Too bad she didn't understand the beauty of a '55 Chevy.

8

THROUGH THE HAZE of gray smoke Emma spotted Brenda standing at the door of Darby's Bar and Grill. Emma did a double take and nearly dropped the tray of drinks she carried for the three rowdy truckers at table four.

What the hell was Brenda doing here? No one knew where Emma worked, except Brenda of course, but she wouldn't...

What the hell *was* she doing here?

Emma craned her neck to see past her friend. She had to be alone. Brenda knew better than to bring anyone here, but still...

"Hey, darlin', you gonna wait until we've died of thirst before you bring that cute little fanny over here?" The guy with the long black beard and gleaming gold tooth winked at her, setting her teeth on edge.

He and his two friends looked out of place, surrounded by yuppie types in Brooks Brothers suits. The usual lunch crowd was made up of young lawyers and paralegals, businessmen from the high-rise down the street, and a few doctors who worked at the emergency care clinic on the corner.

She balanced the tray of drinks in one hand, and

started passing out the bottles of beer and shots of tequila with the other. "You guys want menus?"

"I do," the one with long straight blond hair that hung in his eyes said, and Emma peered closer at his youthful face, wondering if she should card him.

"Hey, Lyle, I think she's sweet on you." The other two chuckled like twelve-year-olds when the blond kid blushed.

Emma glanced toward the doorway, but Brenda had already taken a seat at the end of the bar. Of all the rotten days for Brenda to visit. Usually the place was nice and quiet, catering mostly to regulars, who tipped generously.

"What'll it be, guys?" She switched the tray to her other hand. She ached from the tips of her fingers all the way down to her toes. "I don't have all day."

"Why? You getting off work soon?" Gold tooth grinned mischievously at her.

She sighed with relief. That one look spoke volumes. These guys were harmless. After waitressing for four years, she knew the type. Annoying, but not a threat.

She gave them her best no-nonsense look. "One last chance— You want menus?"

"That depends." Gold tooth picked up his shot glass and downed it. "You on it?"

"That's an old, tired line. You should be ashamed of yourself for even using it." She turned to Lyle. "The fish and chips and Reuben are both really good, but I'll get you a menu."

"Bring me one, too," the third guy said.

She gave gold tooth a brief, expectant glance.

He squinted at her. "Haven't we met before?"

She tossed back her hair and smiled sweetly. "Probably. I'm the part-time receptionist at the VD clinic."

Lyle nearly spit out his beer.

The third guy howled with laughter. "That was pretty good, Norm. You gotta give her credit for that one." He dragged the back of his hand across the dampness in his eyes. "Sweetheart, bring me another beer with that menu."

Norm didn't look as though he wanted to give her anything but a hard time.

Emma spun away, anxious to fill their orders and have them get on their way. She quickly got menus and beer, at the same time waving acknowledgement at Brenda.

Most of the lunch crowd had already left and she had only a half an hour left in her shift. She checked on her last two tables and was glad when they asked for their checks.

After settling up with them and taking the truckers' orders, she slid onto a bar stool next to Brenda. "What are you doing here?"

"I was in the neighborhood."

"Yeah, right. You've never in your life been this far south of Raleigh." One of the reasons Emma took the job, she wouldn't bump into anyone she knew.

Brenda stared at Emma's chest. "I had no idea you had that much cleavage."

"I don't. It's one of those booster things."

"How did you get it on under that skimpy... whatever?"

"I didn't. It's built in." Emma made a face at the

red satin teddy-like outfit. "Did you come all the way over here to tell me how tacky I look?"

Brenda snorted. "Tacky? You look incredible. You don't even look like you."

"Thanks."

"I meant it as a compliment."

Emma tossed back her hair. It was terribly inconvenient to leave it down, but tips did pay her tuition. "The minute I can say adios to this job won't be a second too soon."

Brenda glanced at the trio of truckers. "You must get a lot of hassle."

"Not really. Most of the customers are regulars." She stared at Brenda. Something was wrong. She seemed nervous, unusually fidgety. "You haven't told me why you're here."

"I've tried calling you several times during the past few days, but you haven't been home, and your answering machine isn't picking up."

Emma sighed. "It's broken." Yet another thing she couldn't afford to fix or replace. "I still can't believe you came all this way."

"I was worried that you went back to Utah."

That startled Emma. True, her mother did have a habit of calling Emma for every little thing, but she'd only gone back twice since she'd met Brenda. "Nick could have told you I was still here."

"He's not exactly speaking to me."

She laughed. "You're kidding?"

Brenda shook her head, her brows drawn together in a troubled frown. "He thinks—" She stopped short and bit her lip. "Never mind. Anyway, what I wanted to ask you—"

"Em, your order's up," Manny hollered from the kitchen.

She slid off the stool, muttering an oath. "I've asked him a dozen times not to yell like that. I'll be right back."

As soon as her feet hit the floor her arches started to ache. Two double shifts in a row on high heels were killing her. The first thing she was going to do when she got home was get into a hot bath, and then put her feet up for the rest of the evening.

She delivered two cheeseburgers, a Reuben and three orders each of coleslaw and onion rings to the truckers' table, and then got them another round of drinks. They were obviously hungry because they started digging in instead of giving her any more lip.

While taking their empty glasses to the bar, she gave Brenda a sideways glance. Her friend's gaze roamed every nook and cranny of the room. Emma couldn't imagine what she thought of the place, or of Emma's uniform, for that matter.

She still didn't know what was so darn important that Brenda would come all this way. Unless it had something to do with Nick. Was he backing out of the study? Had he sent Brenda to do his dirty work?

Her pulse skidded and her throat got tight. If that was the case, Emma was royally screwed. No way could she find someone else and then start over.

And Nick. There'd be no reason to see him again.

Two of the dirty glasses slid off her tray and hit the tile floor, shattering, and startling everyone into silence. Quickly she stooped to pick up the pieces of glass. When Brenda started to get up to help, Emma waved her to sit back down.

Stupid, stupid, stupid.

She deserved to have to clean up by herself. Nick was a test subject, period. She had no business having the remotest interest in him. Sure, he was good-looking, witty, smart. That was part of his charm. That was why women were attracted to him. Good reasons Emma couldn't afford to be.

They had zero in common, not that she was even in his league. He wasn't even a willing subject. Brenda had somehow bribed him. And at times, he was only marginally cooperative. But, dammit, he'd gotten to her from the beginning...when he'd called her Doc.

She recalled that first day with perfect clarity. How he'd encouraged her to act and think in terms of her vision. Silly for her to take his general philosophy so personally, she knew, especially since he hadn't even known her, but she'd gotten so little positive feedback in her life that she'd soaked up his encouragement like a thirsty sponge.

She glanced up and saw Brenda staring at her with an anxious expression, probably wondering if Emma had decided to camp out on the floor. Straightening slowly, she felt every muscle and tendon from the arches of her feet to her thighs tighten and scream. What she wouldn't give to have her hands around the neck of the idiot who invented high heels.

After disposing of the broken glass, she grabbed the broom. A quick sweep would do it, and then she could go find out what was bothering Brenda.

STILL BLOWN AWAY by her friend's stunningly sexy look, Brenda watched Emma clean up. Spiked black heels, black hose, the tight red satin camisole...and holy smokes, she had no idea Em had legs. Not like those. She couldn't remember ever seeing her in anything but pants, and once she'd seen Emma's hair in a ponytail, but never down.

The pub was a surprise, too. It was nicely decorated and upscale, the booths a rich burgundy leather and the brass along the bar gleaming with care. Clearly the place catered to a well-heeled crowd...and the odd rowdy, Brenda thought as she eyed the three guys scarfing down their food. But Em always referred to it as the restaurant. It was undoubtedly a bar. Of course the reason for her vagueness was obvious. This was so not Emma.

Except that she was one of the most determined women Brenda had ever met, and if this was the best way to pay her tuition, then it really was no surprise.

They'd been friends for two years, but they were both busy with school and most of their contact was either on campus or over lunch. She wished they could spend more time together. Tonight would be fun, even though it was about getting Em and Nick together in a social setting. By now sparks should be flying between the two of them.

The mess cleared, Emma reclaimed her seat. "Sorry about that." She shook her head, sighing. "It's been one of those days." Her brows drew together in a worried frown. "Are you here because of Nick?"

"Nick? What do you mean?"

"If you are, I'd rather you just spit it out and get it over with."

"Spit what out?"

Emma blinked. "Okay, maybe I'm jumping to conclusions. Like I said, it's been that kind of day."

Perfect opening. "Sounds like you need a distraction."

"What I need is a hot bath, two aspirin and lots of peace and quiet so I can finish grading papers."

"Boring."

Emma snorted. "This coming from you?"

"Hey, I have a life."

They both laughed.

Brenda blinked. "I need a favor."

"Sure." Em seemed surprised. "Anything. I owe you for delivering Nick."

"I want you to go to a party with me tonight."

"A party?" Emma wrinkled her nose. "Oh, God, please tell me you're kidding."

"I'm not."

"I hate parties."

"So do I. That's why I'm making you go with me."

"Bren," Em drawled out her name. "You're not really..."

"Yep. You need to get out."

"Is that what this is about? Then you came a long way across town for nothing."

"First, I really was in the neighborhood. I'm on the board of the annual Renaissance festival, and we meet about a mile from here. Second, I really, really don't want to go to this party alone."

Emma's look of defeat was reassuring. "What kind of party is this?"

"It's not a sit-down dinner or anything like that.

It's more like a reception with cocktails, hors d'oeuvres, that sort of thing.''

"Yeah, but what's it for?''

"It's one of those charity events for Feed the Homeless. I'm sure you've heard of it.''

Emma seemed slightly mollified. "I doubt I have the right clothes for that sort of thing.''

"It's not dressy. God forbid, that would be mocking the cause.'' Brenda gave her a winning smile even Nick would take notice of. "Come on, Em, I'm sure you have at least one dress. I promise we won't stay long.''

The guy with the beard Emma had served earlier yelled for another beer. Em sighed loudly and slid off the stool. "What time?''

"I'll pick you up at six-fifteen.''

"Great,'' she mumbled, "why couldn't you've twisted Nick's arm instead.''

"Oh, didn't I mention it? He'll be there.''

EMMA SAW HIM near the ornate circular stairway as soon as she walked into the foyer. It didn't matter that the English cottage-style home was monstrous, more of an estate really, belonging to the widow of the once very prominent Malcom Simon. Em's gaze immediately riveted to Nick.

He wore a navy sports coat, white shirt and gray slacks, no tie. His hair looked slightly damp still, and his face was clean-shaven, unlike yesterday when he came to the lab. He was by far the most attractive man in the room, at least to Emma's mind. Half a dozen women agreed with her judging by the way they flocked around him, jockeying for position next to him, touching his arm and laughing.

Emma shook her head. Some breather this turned out to be. She'd purposely called off today's session to give them a break from each other.

"What's wrong?" Brenda sidled up to her and handed her a glass of white wine.

She swung her gaze away from Nick. "Nothing."

"Uh-huh."

"Look, I don't think I'm dressed appropriately. Maybe I'll just—"

"Are you nuts? You look terrific!" The frown of disbelief Brenda gave her should have been flattering, but Em just wanted out. "You couldn't have chosen a better dress for the occasion, or for that body of yours. Damn, girl, I didn't know you had legs like those."

"Knock it off."

Brenda laughed. "I'm just jealous as hell."

"I didn't have any choice," Emma said dryly, and tugged at the too-short hem of the black silk shift. "It's my only dress."

"Really?" The trace of sympathy in her friend's eyes annoyed Emma.

"I have two suits for business meetings or interviews, but you know I prefer pants." Good thing. Clothes were a luxury she couldn't afford. Good thing, too, that nobody knew when you wore the same two pairs of jeans or khakis all the time.

"Well, you look..." Brenda sighed. "Incredible."

Warmth invaded her cheeks and she shrugged. "Thanks."

"Well, shall we mingle?"

"Only if we have to."

"We do. Come on." Brenda took hold of Emma's arm and dragged her off, thankfully, in the opposite direction of Nick.

But as they made their way through the massive foyer into the parlor, Emma thought she saw Nick give them a double take. Made her wonder if he knew she'd be there. Not that it mattered. Why would he care? Why should she?

"I want you to see the gardens out back," Brenda said as she snatched two bacon-wrapped shrimp off the tray of a passing waiter and handed one to Emma. "It's almost an acre of ponds and flowers and rock falls. I was kind of hoping the party would be out there."

"Too chilly."

"Yeah, I suppose." She eyed Emma's sleeveless dress. "Would you rather stay in here?"

Emma gave her a dry look.

"That's what I thought." Brenda stopped, frowned in the direction of the glass doors. "Oh, no, there's Tiffany. Go that way," she said, redirecting them toward the living room.

"Who's Tiffany?"

"Nick's current girlfriend."

Emma stared over her shoulder at the short, slim blond-haired woman who was inspecting her manicure. Several other women in casually elegant dinner dresses were standing around her chatting and sipping from champagne flutes, but Emma instinctively knew which one was Tiffany.

In a deceptively even tone, she said, "I didn't know he had a girlfriend."

Brenda yanked her along. "Quit looking. She'll see me and come over."

Reluctantly, Emma dragged her gaze away from the woman. "I take it you don't like her."

"I haven't formed an opinion yet. I only met her two days ago but I'm not in the mood to make small talk about the latest discoveries in the world of cosmetics."

"Snob."

Brenda's mouth turned up in a wry smile. "Yeah, then you go talk to her."

Emma chuckled, even though she didn't feel like it. That Nick had a girlfriend shouldn't matter in the least. She knew he dated. He reminded her often enough. But somehow, seeing this woman and knowing that she was the one in whom Nick confided, who he held in his arms at night, it got to Emma in a mindless, depressing way that frightened her, and made her suddenly desperate to leave.

What the hell was wrong with her? Nick was simply her test subject, for God's sake. Sure, he'd flirted with her a little bit. But that was just Nick. It wasn't personal.

"What's wrong?" Brenda stopped and stared at her with wide eyes. "You're pale."

"I—I'm not— I think I need to go. I'm not feeling so hot all of a sudden." She swallowed around the lump forming in her throat. "I'm sorry. I think exhaustion is catching up."

Brenda glanced at her empty glass. "Or too much wine."

She hadn't realized she'd downed it. "One glass? I don't think so."

"Let's step outside and get some fresh air. Besides, it'll be too dark to see the garden soon." Brenda grabbed a small plate of munchies, and then steered them toward the French doors off the living room, smiling and nodding toward several people she knew, but never stopping.

Emma had no fight left in her. She really was tired. And what the hell? Outside was good. Away from Nick…away from his girlfriend…away from this well-heeled crowd in which Emma didn't belong.

"Check this out." Brenda pushed open the doors to the terrace.

Flowers in vibrant hues from purple to majestic burgundy stretched endlessly down a gentle slope. Even in her miserable state, Emma's breath caught at the beautiful mixture of colors and textures flowing together. Giant, graceful weeping willows sheltered the pond at the outskirts of the property.

If she'd expected a meticulously manicured garden, she would have been horribly disappointed. Many of the more brilliant sprays looked like wildflowers, creating a magical madness in the way they tangled together like lovers.

"This is…" She shaded her eyes against the setting sun. "Amazing."

Brenda let out a heartfelt sigh. "Screw the white picket fence. I want a garden just like this."

"Ladies, we need everyone to come inside for a few minutes."

Emma and Brenda turned at the same time. A silver-haired woman in a royal blue silk shirtdress stood at the door waving them inside.

"Mrs. Simon, we were just admiring your garden." Brenda started to introduce Emma.

"I don't mean to be rude, dear, but we must hurry. We're about to present our guest of honor with an award." Mrs. Simon gave Emma a smile of apology as she stepped back from the door.

"We're coming." Brenda tilted her head toward Emma. "This shouldn't take long."

Great. Emma briefly wondered if it would be too rude to beg off and stay outside. "I thought you said this was just a cocktail reception."

"It is, but they always present their annual award to the volunteer of the year. I promise it'll only take a few minutes."

"Sure, we'll probably have to listen to some long speech," Emma muttered as Brenda led her inside.

"No way. Nick hates speeches."

Emma stopped dead in her tracks and yanked Brenda back. "Nick?"

"He's the guest of honor." Brenda's expression was innocent enough, except for the spark of mischief in her eyes. "Didn't I mention that?"

9

"ATTENTION EVERYONE." Mrs. Simon tapped the side of her crystal wineglass with a silver cocktail fork. "May I please have everyone's attention for a moment?"

Propped in front of the stone fireplace like a damn centerpiece, Nick glared at the woman. She'd promised him there'd be no big to-do over this award. Shit! A root canal without Novocain would've been preferable to standing here in front of all these people. See if he volunteered for next year's fund drive.

To top it all off, he was pretty sure he'd seen Doc earlier. So what the hell was she doing here? Recalling the glimpse he'd had of her—hair down, that black dress that showed off every damn curve better than he could've fantasized, got his heart pumping faster than an oil rig.

While Mrs. Simon droned on about the importance of volunteerism, Nick scanned the crowd. Just as she handed him the bronze plaque engraved with his name, he spotted Emma.

She stood in the back next to a potted palm, looking as happy to be here as he was. Her hair was down, draping her breasts, the rich brown strands highlighted golden by the waning sun streaming in from the terrace doors.

Her lips were tinted pink, glistening, tempting. And that dress, showing off just the right amount of cleavage—enough to make a grown man cry—was downright lethal.

"Nick?"

He stared blankly at the concern in Mrs. Simon's face. "Yeah?"

Someone coughed. A few others laughed.

Mrs. Simon pressed her lips together but couldn't quite conceal the smile lurking at the corners. "Don't you have anything to say?"

He glanced down at the plaque, and then at the curious and amused faces out in the crowd. He cleared his throat, pushed a hand through his hair. It was still damp. "Yeah, thanks."

More laughter.

He didn't care. All he wanted was to get out of here, and a drink sure as hell wouldn't hurt either. He moved away and headed straight for a tray of champagne.

"Well, since Nick is too modest to speak on his own behalf," Mrs. Simon began. "I'd like to further extend my appreciation for his generous contribution to the shelter and to the people of this city."

Emma watched Nick try to make a run for it. He downed nearly an entire flute of champagne and was heading toward the back of the house before Tiffany caught up with him. He didn't seem pleased that she'd wrapped a hand around his arm and tried to stop him, or that she tried to follow him when he wouldn't be waylaid.

"Most of you don't realize," Mrs. Simon was saying, "that Nick doesn't only donate a goodly portion of his own money, but he gives a considerable amount of his time to the shelter. Currently he is working on developing a small business that would employ many of our city's homeless men and women with all profit generated going to the shelter.''

The crowd applauded and started looking around to see where Nick had gone.

He looked angry, standing in the back, Tiffany still plastered to his side. He made a slashing motion with his hand across his throat, clearly telling Mrs. Simon to cut off the speech.

If she noticed, she chose to ignore him and continued extolling his virtues. He shook off Tiffany and left through the terrace doors.

''Uh-oh. Nick is pissed,'' Brenda whispered. ''He's into doing things anonymously. I'm going to go find him. I'll be back.''

Emma nodded, feeling helpless, resisting the urge to follow and soothe Nick herself. Except she had no right. He wouldn't welcome her interference. She edged closer to the terrace doors, unsure what she hoped to accomplish. Mrs. Simon had cooled it on the personal things Nick had done for the shelter and gone on to other business, but Emma had already heard enough about the man to surprise her.

Two middle-aged women stood near the door talking, sipping from their flutes of champagne and sliding glances outside, apparently interested in what had happened to Nick. Emma had gotten close enough that she couldn't help but hear their conversation.

''What do you suppose has gotten into him?'' the redhead with the enormous diamond earrings asked. ''Nick is usually so...charming and polite.''

"I don't know." Her more conservatively dressed companion frowned with concern. "But he doesn't like being spotlighted in any way. I have a feeling he didn't know Esther was going to deliver a dissertation on his personal involvement with the shelter."

"Oh, well, the boy should be properly recognized. Not many young men his age are concerned with anything or anyone but themselves."

"All his charity work is certainly commendable, but what he should be working on is getting married and starting a family."

That startled a laugh out of Emma, netting her sharp looks from both women. "Hello," she said lamely and started to move on.

"Wait. I don't believe we've met."

She'd already turned away and wasn't sure which woman had spoken, but since the one with the diamonds wasn't smiling, Emma addressed herself to the other woman. "I'm Emma Snow."

Both women looked blankly at her and she supposed they were waiting for elaboration but she didn't feel like making small talk with strangers.

"A friend of Nick's?" the woman persisted when Emma started to leave again.

The redhead laughed. "Isn't every woman?"

"No," Emma said with a sweet smile. "Some women think he's full of hot air."

The blonde gasped, her eyes widening in disbelief, but she couldn't be half as shocked as Emma that such an impolite remark had come out of her mouth. She had no idea what had gotten into her. Maybe she was just sick of women fawning over him. Not that that was any kind of excuse.

"I'm sorry," she said quickly. "I've had a bad day. I'm sorry for my abhorrent manners."

The other woman's coral-colored lips curved in an amused smile. "I'm afraid my manners are also lacking. I'm Catherine Ryder. Nick's mother." She extended her hand, an odd curiosity lighting her eyes.

And here Emma thought the day couldn't get worse. Damn it all to hell. She accepted the woman's hand. Her grasp was warm and firm. "Excuse me, please. I need to step outside and smother myself."

Mortified, Emma didn't wait for a response but slipped out the door. It was a big garden. She didn't have to run into Nick and Brenda. She gulped in the cool air, grateful for the descending duskiness, too rattled to appreciate the ribbon of pink and salmon just beyond the weeping willows, remnants of a Chapel Hill sunset.

The air was too cool to be outside in a sleeveless dress, but it felt good on her face and neck where the heat of embarrassment lingered.

Nick's mother.

Emma sighed loudly. Dammit. Of all people for her to be flip with. At least this was it. The evening couldn't possibly get worse.

"What are you doing out here?"

Nick's voice, low and gruff, came from the shadows.

Emma jumped and spun toward the sound. "Don't sneak up on me like that."

"What's the matter, Doc? Afraid of the dark?"

She squinted but could only see part of his outline. "Where's Brenda?"

"Ah, so it's me you're afraid of. Come on, Doc.

Didn't all those good people convince you what a nice guy I am?"

"What's gotten into you—" She saw a small red glow. "You're smoking?"

He didn't answer.

"I didn't know you smoked."

"I don't."

"What's that, a sparkler?" Her sarcasm was undermined when a chill made her shiver. She wrapped her arms around herself.

Nick snorted. "Hell, Doc, if you're gonna come out and bother me, you need to at least keep warm."

"I didn't come out to see you. I slipped out because—because I..." Her sigh was equally loud. "Because I opened my big mouth and stuck my foot in it, and I needed some air."

He chuckled and moved forward, enough that she could see half his face. The intense way he looked at her made her shiver again.

"Come here." He shrugged out of his sports coat.

"You keep it on. I'm fine."

"You're on my turf now, Doc." He smiled as he ground out the cigarette, and then pulled her toward him.

She stumbled a little on the uneven stones and put her palms against his chest to steady herself.

"Now you're getting in the spirit of things, Doc." He put an arm around her before she could protest.

Disappointment swelled when she realized he only meant to place the coat around her shoulders. "Thank you," she said stiffly, and jerked her shoulder away from his touch.

He was quick. Grabbing the loose coat sleeves, he drew her back toward him.

"What are you doing?" She swept a glance around. They were completely alone. From inside she could hear music and laughter.

"You smell good, Doc." He pulled her so close her breasts rubbed his chest. "Damn good."

"You smell like an ashtray."

He stiffened slightly, and then he chuckled, the movement of his lips tickling the side of her neck. "Nice try. I only had half a cigarette."

"I still don't like it."

His hand moved down the side of her waist, glided over her hip, and she held her breath. He reached into the pocket of his coat. "Help me open this."

She glanced down. He held a roll of breath mints. "You have two hands."

"How observant, Doc." He let go of the jacket sleeve. "Problem is, one of them is occupied," he said as he slipped beneath the coat and splayed his hand across her rib cage, his thumb brushing the under part of her breast.

Her breath caught in a painful knot in her chest and she tried to shove back.

"Please, Doc." His hand slackened. "Don't go."

If his voice hadn't lowered, if he hadn't sounded so earnest, she might have turned and run. But something was different about him tonight. Something that stirred more than her curiosity. "Why were you smoking?"

He sighed and dropped his hand altogether. "Half a cigarette. Big deal."

"You claim you don't smoke."

"Shit, Doc." He shrugged away and stared out at the semidark garden. "Don't start that analyzing crap."

"Nick." She crossed her arms and pulled the jacket tighter around her shoulders. His musky scent rose from the fabric and drugged her already intoxicated senses.

"I've probably had the sum total of one pack of cigarettes in my entire life. Occasionally, when I have a drink, I have a cigarette. End of story."

"Okay," she said softly, deciding they weren't going to get anywhere with this conversation.

He turned and raised an eyebrow at her. "Okay?"

"Sure, I can be reasonable."

He laughed quietly and then stared out toward the faint pink glow along the horizon. "Hell, it's still light enough. Come here." He held out a hand. "I want to show you something."

"Out there?" Emma squinted at the chaos of flowers and shrubs with more than a little skepticism.

"Come on. I know you're not a wuss."

"Being a wuss has nothing to do with it. It's getting dark. Plus I've got on high heels."

"Amen to that." He grinned down at her legs. "Doc, you have no business having such great wheels."

She made a sound of exasperation even though his compliment gave her a warm rush of pleasure. "Wheels? Don't be a pig."

Laughing, he opened the roll of mints and popped one into his mouth. He held them out to her. "Want one?"

"No, thanks—well, maybe I will."

One side of his mouth lifted, and she bit back the urge to tell him wanting a breath mint had absolutely nothing to do with kissing. Assuming that's what he was thinking. Of course it was.

She chomped into the mint and caught the inside of her cheek. Dammit.

"Ready?"

"For?"

"It's just a short walk, Doc."

She hesitated. She supposed she should ask what he could possibly show her in the growing darkness, but the truth was, she wanted to go with him. Anyway, how much could he have in mind? He still called her Doc.

He tugged on her hand. "Come on. If you scream a dozen people will come to your rescue."

"But since they seem to think you're God's gift to us mere mortals, they'd probably—" She trailed off when he dropped her hand and abruptly turned away. Though not before she saw the irritation in his face.

"It was a joke, Nick."

"Yeah, I know." He shrugged. "Forget it."

She touched his arm. "What you do for the shelter and the community, I think is really—"

He turned and stopped her with a finger to her lips. "There are ground rules to this excursion. No talking about me."

She drew her head back in mock surprise. "And I thought we lived in a democracy."

"Scratch that. No talking, period."

"If you think—"

His mouth silenced her this time. It came down so fast, she didn't have time to react. She just stood there, half stunned, half aroused and entirely uncertain.

She did her best not to respond to the pressure building against her lips, the tugging and nibbling and licking that were making her slightly light-headed. He used his tongue to trace the seam of her lips, teasing, prodding, inspiring wicked thoughts. Mint and champagne mingled on his warm breath, making for a heady combination that undermined her common sense.

She didn't know exactly when she put her hand on his shoulder, or slipped her arm around his neck. But when the friction of her breasts rubbing against his chest started a pool of moisture between her thighs, lightning struck and she jerked away.

Caught off balance, his arms tightened around her. "Ah, Emma, don't run away." His voice was barely above a whisper, hoarse, raspy.

The way he'd said her name made her go boneless. The way his arousal swelled against her belly forced her to move back and quell the shiver building at the base of her spine.

What the hell was she doing? This behavior was inexcusable. He was her test subject. She couldn't afford to color her results now.

She took a deep breath. The first attempt didn't work. She tried again, and then exhaled slowly, quietly. "What did you want to show me?"

He stared silently at her. It was too dark to make out his features, but facing the illumination of the house as she was, she knew he could see hers. She huddled deeper into his coat and turned away.

"Cold?" he asked, raising his hand to touch her cheek.

"What did you want to show me?" she repeated.

He lowered his hand. "What if I told you I only wanted to get you out here alone?"

"I'd say that would piss off your girlfriend."

"My girlfriend?" He paused. "Tiffany?"

Emma didn't say anything.

Nick snorted. "Is that what Brenda told you?"

"You've mentioned her name yourself." Using the sleeves, she pulled the jacket tighter around herself. It felt decadently intimate, as if they were his arms holding her, squeezing her tighter. If that's what she wanted, all she had to do was take a step forward...

"I just started seeing her two weeks ago, and I may have mentioned I had a date with her, but we don't see each other exclusively. I don't see *anyone* exclusively."

"I'm sure you don't," she muttered, annoyed that she sounded so tart. She shouldn't be having this conversation, much less have an opinion about Nick's dating habits.

"I don't hide that fact," he said, defensiveness clear in his voice. "Not from any woman I date. As far as Tiffany is concerned, even if I wanted to see her exclusively she'd think I was trying to cramp her style."

"I didn't mean to offend you."

He chuckled. "Come here. Let's sit down."

She shook her head. Was it because she was overly tired, or was he being weird? "There's no place to sit."

"Sure, there is. Right here by the pond."

"I can't see anything."

"Then you'll have to trust me." He held out his hand to her.

"This may amaze you but there are chairs in the house. People actually sit on them."

"Ah, there's the rub. They come with people. Me, I like it out here where it's nice and quiet."

A frog croaked right at that moment, and Emma jumped. She uttered a mild oath that made Nick laugh. "Okay, I'm out of here."

"Come on, Doc." He grabbed her hand, preventing escape. "Where's your sense of adventure?"

It was silly, but she regretted that he'd reverted to Doc. It probably should've been reassuring. "I save it for the daytime when I can see what I'm getting into."

He cupped her nape with his large warm palm. "What are you afraid of, Doc?"

"Nothing."

"Nothing at all?" His voice had lowered again, sending goose bumps stampeding up her arms.

"Not you."

His laugh was low and throaty. Damn him. "Prove it. Come sit with me."

She hesitated, and he tugged at her hand. She took a few cautious steps and saw the pond, the shimmering pool of water much larger than she'd expected. It looked more like a lake. Of course in Nick's world, everything seemed to be bigger and better.

Thankfully, he didn't go far before he started to lower himself to the ground. "There's a flat rock here we can sit on," he said, motioning to a slab that jutted out a little over the water.

It wasn't so dark that she couldn't see the area was small...too small. "There isn't enough room for both of us."

"Sure, there is." He sat as far back as he could. "You sit here." He patted the spot between his spread legs.

"Oh, yeah, sure thing."

"Chicken."

"That has nothing to do with it." Lying wasn't necessarily bad in this instance. "I'll ruin my dress."

"Use my coat to sit on."

"Then I'll ruin *it*."

"You are chicken." His tone implied the idea amazed him. Ha! Like she didn't know that trick.

"Cut the act. It won't work." She lifted her chin. She wouldn't let him goad her. "I'm practical. That's all."

"Uh-huh." He picked up a small, flat stone and skipped it across the water's surface.

"Think what you want."

"I doubt you'd like me to do that." His voice was husky again, leaving no room for idle interpretation.

Behind her, the music and laughter from inside the house seeped out when someone opened the door to the terrace. She turned but could only see the outline of a man and woman.

"Shit," Nick muttered. "Come on, Doc, sit down before someone sees you and comes sticking their nose out here."

She thought about it only for a second, and then took the hand he offered and lowered her butt to the rock with an unladylike thud. She didn't care. Better that than someone seeing them outside together. Alone. In the dark.

"Your eagerness is flattering." Nick chuckled and wrapped an arm around the front of her shoulders to pull her back against him. "You're stiff. Relax."

What the hell was she doing, besides blatantly asking for trouble? "I'm going back to the house."

His other arm came around and crossed over her, imprisoning her, his elbow resting at the top of her breast. "Look at the moon."

"Where?" It was hard to breathe, much less move or speak. Yet it felt oddly soothing to be snuggled up against him. The way he cradled her back and lightly rested his arms around her offered comfort and companionship.

But she wasn't fooled that if she gave him the slightest encouragement, if she so much as turned her head to give him permission, he'd swoop down like a hawk. The idea gave her an inappropriate thrill.

"Look, behind the willows." He pointed and ducked his head so that his jaw grazed her temple. "It's a crescent. See?"

His skin was already slightly beard-roughened, and his musky scent made her want to snuggle closer, turn her head that extra inch.

"Nick?"

"Hmm?"

"We shouldn't be here."

"Why not?" His arms tightened ever so slightly and his breath stirred her hair as he made a quiet sound of contentment.

"Not like this."

"Isn't it nice to not have a desk between us? We're

just two people sharing a moon. We aren't doing anything wrong, Emma.''

But she wanted to. That was the problem. ''It's just not professional.''

''Good, that's my point. This is a social occasion, nothing professional about it.''

''You know what I mean.''

''I won't lie. I'm glad to get you alone like this. Away from the lab where I'm not your guinea pig. I like you and I think you like me.'' He paused as if looking for confirmation. She said nothing. ''No reason we can't just be two people who are attracted to each other.''

''It doesn't work that way. Tomorrow we'll have another session and—'' His lips were too close to her ear, his warm breath tickling something deep inside her, making her want to give in. ''Later, maybe, after the study.'' She bit her lower lip. She shouldn't have said that.

''Look at me.''

She stiffened, but couldn't deny the excitement building in her belly, traveling to all points north and south. ''Why?''

He shifted, angling his body, and guiding her chin toward him. ''For this.''

His lips touched hers so gently it was frustrating. He drew back a little, but then slanted his mouth against hers and tasted with more urgency. His hand slid to her breast and he cupped her with such quiet reverence it made her shiver.

''Nick,'' she whispered, weak and unconvincing. ''I'm serious. We shouldn't—'' She moaned when his hand retreated, and then through the light silk fabric, he rubbed only her nipple. It budded immediately, greedy for more of his touch.

She squirmed and whimpered, horrified the sound came from her mouth.

It only fueled Nick. He covered her breast with his hand, using the center of his palm to create unbearable friction. He'd slid his other hand up her leg where the hem of her dress rode up on her thigh.

"Emma, kiss me." His voice was so ragged she barely heard him. He sucked her lower lip into his mouth, and then sought her tongue with his.

She wanted to dive in with him, get lost in the heat and insanity that was making her needy and foolish. They'd gone this far already. A line had been crossed. What would it matter if…?

"Nick? Is that you?"

A low-pitched feminine voice came from behind them.

Emma blinked away the fog and tried to quell the rising panic in her chest as she tugged down her dress. A circle of light shined directly into their faces, blinding her.

Nick sighed and sank back against the rocks. "Hello, Tiffany."

10

NICK HAD ALWAYS MADE IT A RULE to never play with fire. He stuck to that principle no matter what, even if it meant brutal honesty, buckets of dreaded female tears or moving on from a relationship that had been relatively satisfying. So what the hell had he done last night?

He sat in the psych lab's parking lot and stared at the small white building. The torture chamber. That's what today would feel like, torture, sitting across from her, staring into her anxious hazel eyes, remembering how her breast fit so perfectly in his hand, how the touch of her lips alone gave him an instant hard-on.

The thought of having to see her again should have put a bad taste in his mouth. Especially so soon after last night's disaster. Hell, he couldn't wait.

Shit!

He got out of the Porsche and stretched. His back and neck ached. Too much tossing and turning last night. If he'd gotten any decent sleep at all, his dreams probably would've been whoppers.

The idea of using another *Midnight Fantasy* reader's letter today did make him wonder if he'd totally lost his mind.

Things were heated enough between them. Hell, he didn't know if he could get the entire story out without totally blowing it, or laying her across the desk, spreading her thighs and tasting her honey.

His blood pumped faster.

Maybe she'd be ready for him. Maybe with the combination of last night's foreplay and the erotic tale he'd tell today, she'd welcome him.

Excitement stirred in his belly, tightened his jeans. She had the most incredible lips of any woman he'd ever run across. Fleeting images of what those lips could do to him haunted him, made him think about getting back in his car.

But a sudden recollection of the humiliation that burned in her face last night cooled him down. He'd give anything to have erased her embarrassment. He shouldn't have pushed, but respected her reluctance. Good thing Tiffany hadn't caused a scene. That would've been the end of it for sure.

He froze in the middle of pocketing his keys.

The end of what?

Nothing was going on between him and Doc. Nothing at all. She'd never given him the come-on, and she certainly hadn't leaped at the chance to go see his Chevy. For his part, he found her funny and smart, and sexy in spite of those ugly black glasses she hid behind. Of course he was interested. Just not seriously.

Glasses.

It finally hit him. She hadn't been wearing them last night. He grunted. A sexy dress and no glasses. That meant something.

He finished stuffing his keys in his pocket and then realized he hadn't locked the Porsche. Hesitating, he glanced in the window. Nothing worth stealing, only the plaque he'd received last night was stuck between the console and the passenger seat.

Damn that Esther Simon. She'd promised no fanfare.

He never minded donating time, money or know-how to a good cause, but he detested attracting attention. Everyone he'd ever worked with knew that, and of all times for Mrs. Simon to get stupid, and do it in front of Emma.

He left the car unlocked and crossed the parking lot, craning his neck to see if her car was parked on the side. He couldn't tell, but he was only five minutes early. She was probably already inside.

In fact, she was sitting at her desk when he opened the door. Ugly black glasses in place. Hair pulled into a bun. The big white shirt hiding her perfect breasts.

She glanced up, unsmiling, and blinked.

"Hi, Doc."

"Hello." She seemed stiff and formal, and he hated it.

Sighing, he slumped into his usual chair across from her.

"Don't turn the recorder on yet," he said when it looked as though she was reaching for the button.

"Okay," she said calmly, and chose a red-colored pencil out of the Far Side mug behind the recorder.

He wondered what that cherry red would look like on her lips. "We need to talk."

Wariness crept into her eyes, then denial and finally acceptance. "I guess so."

"I'm sorry I embarrassed you."

Surprise registered in her face and then she blinked. "I don't recall you twisting my arm." Her lashes lowered a second. "We both had a slip in judgment. But I can put it behind me if you can."

"Speak for yourself."

She frowned. "Excuse me?"

"I didn't have a slip in judgment. I'm not sorry I kissed you, or that I wanted to do a lot more with you. I regret that we were rudely interrupted with that damn flashlight shining in our faces. What I regret most of all was that you were embarrassed by it."

"What about Tiffany?"

He shrugged. "What about her?"

Her face tightened with disapproval.

"You think I'm being callous because you don't understand our relationship."

"But she was your date. That alone—"

"No, she wasn't. I would never have taken anyone to a reception like that. Esther Simon had invited her."

"Still..." She shook her head, clearly unconvinced, and then gave him a sudden frown. "What do you mean you wouldn't take anyone to a reception like that?"

"Why would I bore a date with that kind—"

"Stop it," she said, cutting him off with an angry glint in her eyes. "Last night was an honor and you'd be a jerk not to accept the acknowledgment."

Anger churned in his gut. "That's not the topic of our discussion."

"Tough."

He snorted at the stubborn lift of her chin. "It's no big deal, Doc. I have the time and resources. It's not like I'm making any sacrifices."

She stared silently at him with a look he was beginning to recognize. She was trying to figure him out. Get inside his head.

"Dammit, Doc, don't think just because we stuck our tongues in each other's mouths you know me. You don't."

She didn't bat an eye at his choice of words but gave him that serene smile that annoyed him just as much as that measuring look. "Better and easier to give than to receive, isn't it?"

"Keep it up. If you recall, I have a very effective way of shutting you up."

Confusion drew her brows together, making her look sweet and naive. But then understanding dawned, and she glared back. Slowly she rose from her chair, her intention unclear by her blank expression.

She rounded the corner of the desk and said, "Maybe I like the way you shut me up." She shrugged in that coy, feminine way that let a man know he was in trouble. "Maybe I want to..."

Holy shit.

He straightened. She was going to kiss him. Just the thought got his southern hemisphere thinking, expecting, stiffening...

She walked past him.

"You want a bottle of water, I assume," she called matter-of-factly over her shoulder as she disappeared into the back room.

Nick shook his head, mopped his forehead. He'd actually started to sweat. Who knew what kind of anxious expression had been on his face. The little witch was probably back there laughing.

"Sure," he called out, beginning to smile when he

remembered what he had in store for her. "You might want to bring yourself an extra one."

She appeared in the next second and handed him the Evian, her suspicious gaze narrowed. "Don't hold your breath waiting for me to ask what that means."

"I'm guessing a smart girl like you has already figured it out."

"Girl?"

"Just a figure of speech, sweetheart."

"Go ahead, dig yourself in deeper." She sat down and twisted off the bottle cap.

She was awfully cool today. Not what he'd expected. He eyed her for a moment. "By the way, you were right last night. We shouldn't have been getting down and dirty by the pond."

She half sighed, half huffed. "I wouldn't have called it that."

"We should've gone straight to my place. No interruptions there."

She rolled her gaze toward the ceiling and then focused on setting the recorder. "Shall we get started with our session?"

"Sure, Doc, anything you want." He noticed her fingers tremble as she fussed with the recorder. So she wasn't as cool as she pretended. For some reason, that didn't console him.

"Ready?"

He nodded, forcing her to look up again.

She pressed the record button and then settled back with the pencil in her hand. It was fairly steady now.

"Okay, let's see, how did it start?" He looked up quickly, at his slip. She didn't seem concerned. It was his guilty conscience working on him.

"You did take notes? Maybe even did the diagram we discussed?"

"Notes," he muttered, and dug into his pocket for the illegible pages. He'd scribbled the highlights of the story at the last minute. Nevertheless, he straightened out the crumpled paper. "Okay, I was at this party. It was daytime, late afternoon and we were at a lake."

"We?"

"These two girls—"

"Of course."

"Are you going to let me tell this?"

She pushed her glasses into place. "Sorry, I didn't mean to interrupt."

He cleared his throat. "Okay, so we were at this lake, having a few beers, barbecuing, the regular outdoor party stuff that goes on— What?"

Her eyebrows were raised in that scolding schoolmarm look. "You're not giving me enough details."

"Oh, don't worry, I will." He made it sound like a threat.

She sighed. "You know what I mean. Do you actually know the women? Is the lake familiar?"

"If I know, I'll tell you. Otherwise assume this is all anonymous, and we can get through this quicker."

Emma bit back the retort that nearly sprang from her lips. Why the hell was he in such a hurry? Was he late for a date with Tiffany?

After last night, Emma knew this would be a tough session. Acting cool and indifferent helped, but inside her nervous system was working overtime. She'd replayed his kisses a hundred times, ran the palms of her hands over her thighs, her breasts, anyplace he'd touched, wondering what her body felt like to his experienced hands.

Her reaction had been so insane and juvenile it should have been laughable. But she hadn't laughed. She'd been too confused and self-pitying. Thank goodness she'd finally pulled herself together. She couldn't allow what happened to compromise her study. When it was all over, and she'd written her thesis, well…

Well nothing. Nick would be gone, moved on to his next distraction, and she'd be busy working her butt off to settle a mountain of student loans. Sometimes life sucked. But it was the only one she had, and crying over lost opportunities wouldn't get her anywhere. God forbid, it would land her back in Utah, where her mother would eventually leech the life out of her.

"Okay?" He sounded impatient, probably because she hadn't answered him the first time.

"Fine." She didn't even know what he'd said, but she forced herself to concentrate as objectively as possible.

"So we'd all been partying hard, drinking too much and getting daring, when one of the girls decided she wanted to go swimming. Only no one had brought their swimsuits. So she started taking off her clothes. The others whistled and egged her on."

"Others? I thought there were only three of you."

"That's because you interrupted." His gaze lingered on her mouth long enough to make it go dry.

She swallowed. "Who were the others?"

"This is really hard."

"You've forgotten?" That was a surprise. He usually had excellent recall. "Go ahead and check your notes."

"I want to kiss you." His gaze slowly left her mouth to meet her eyes. "I thought I could walk in here and forget about last night."

"You have to," she said, resenting the betraying flutter in her stomach. "We have work to do."

"Maybe if we got in one really good, tonsil-licking kiss along with all the condiments I'd be able to get it out of my system and concentrate."

A nervous laugh escaped her. "Condiments?" She took in a quick breath and held up her hand. "No, I don't want to know. No kissing, no touching. Out of the question."

"Even if it'll help my concentration?"

"Nick, stop it."

He slumped, hunching his shoulders forward slightly like a sulking child. "Why?"

She groaned with exasperation.

"One kiss. What's wrong with that? It shouldn't last more than…" He shrugged, one side of his mouth lifting. "An hour."

She jerked in surprise. Whether from his teasing or the fact that she was tempted, she didn't know which. "Maybe we should resume this session tomorrow."

"Great. That leaves me free for the next two hours." His sexy grin finished the suggestion.

"Nick, please."

His smile vanished, and he stared at her for a moment, regret in his dark eyes. "Let's finish."

She nodded, curious as to what suddenly changed his mood. She dared not ask though. If he was willing to continue, she didn't want to ruin things by getting personal again.

"Let's see…yeah, there were a few other people. I'm not sure how many, maybe four or five, at least one of them another woman, but they're kind of hazy. They didn't do much in the dream except watch."

Oh, brother. She knew it would go in this direction. Why hadn't she switched on the air conditioner?

"Okay, so this blonde took off her T-shirt and bra, and then her shorts. All the guys started chanting for her to take off her panties, but she only laughed and then jumped into the water." He paused, his frown thoughtful, but a smile definitely lurked. "I almost forgot the details. You probably want to know about the woman's body."

"Only if it's important."

"Well, Doc, let's say she kind of took center stage for a while."

"Right." She took a sip of water.

"The thing I remember most is that she had nice round breasts. Not too big but just right. About so." He cupped his hands over his chest, his gaze idly wandering toward her breasts. "About your size, in fact."

The heat immediately flooded the base of her throat, and then rushed to her cheeks. She said nothing. She doubted she could force anything coherent out of her mouth. Especially now that he stared at it again.

"Anyway, she was tan, all over, and really buff like she worked out a lot. And she had great legs just like you."

That innocent smile of his tempted her more than

anything else—to wipe it from his smug face. Instead, she carefully maintained a blank expression and waited for him to continue.

"She got out of the water and you could tell she was really eating up the attention she was getting from everyone. She put on a show by slowly stripping off her panties, which were wet and clinging to her and not hiding a damn thing anyway. Once she was totally naked, she started some stretching and bending exercises, exposing some interesting places.

"All the attention she was getting must have pissed off the other two women because they stripped off their clothes, too, each one making a production of the routine. One had large breasts with nipples that stuck out so far they looked unnatural, as if she were constantly aroused. Which the way she started acting pretty much confirmed."

He paused to pick up the Evian, taking his sweet time to twist off the cap.

"Need help with that?"

"Anxious for me to continue?" he shot back.

No way she'd take the bait. "I was hoping to complete my thesis in this century." It took all her self-control not to make a crass remark about his perverted dreams. That would be real professional.

"Chill out, Doc. I won't keep you hanging." He smiled, and then took a long slow sip of water, while she bit her tongue. "This other woman with the...did I tell you she had two nipple rings on each breast? Two each. That's how much her nipples stuck out." He frowned thoughtfully. "Maybe that's why they stuck out so much, because they were really out to…"

Emma drew his wandering attention with three impatient taps of her pencil.

"Right," he said with an apologetic tone and a devilish gleam in his eye. "Okay, she stood in the middle of everyone, playing with her breasts with these long red nails, and asked if anyone had sucked a nipple ring before. All the guys went nuts, volunteering their service, when she turned to the blonde and asked her if she had.

"The other woman was taken aback at first but she accepted the challenge and approached the brunette. By now everyone else was pulling off their clothes, their eyes glued to the women. The blonde really got into the spirit by ordering the brunette to take off her shorts and then to lie down. She eagerly obeyed, spreading her legs so that we could all see she was completely shaved. Hope this much detail doesn't offend you, Doc."

She shook her head, aware of how intently he watched her, not missing a single reaction or nuance of one. "Go ahead."

"The two of them were really getting into it and of course all the guys cheered them on, but I just sat back, sipping a beer, watching but not participating. I was the only one who still had on clothes. That's probably what got to the brunette because she pointed to me and demanded that I go to her. The blonde had been suckling her and then tried to move her mouth lower.

"But the other woman stopped her and said she was saving that course for me. I didn't know what to say. I just stood there while the blonde tore off my clothes. The brunette played with her nipple rings while she laid back and watched. I was getting pretty horny by then and it didn't take much to encourage me to kneel down between her legs. I was rock hard by then and just as I lowered my mouth, the blonde grasped the base of my—''

Emma's pencil snapped. She jumped and stared down at the stub left in her hand.

"Take it easy, Doc. I haven't even gotten to the good part yet.''

The quiet laughter in his eyes sobered her. She took a deep breath. "Are you sure this was a dream?''

He seemed momentarily disconcerted. "What? You think I made this up?''

"Did you?''

"Doc, you wound me. I thought we were getting to be...friends.''

His subtle but suggestive tone irked her. She took off her glasses and rubbed her weary eyes. Residual mascara and liner from last night smeared her fingertips.

Last night.

What a mistake. Half an hour's lapse in judgment and everything had changed. If she got through this study objectively it would be a miracle.

"What's the matter, Doc?'' he asked quietly. "I'm not scaring you, am I?''

"No, Nick, you're not scaring me. You're pissing me off.'' Unmoved, she stared at the surprise in his face. "You must have a dozen women waiting in line to go out with you...do anything you want. But you obviously have the need to harass me. Why?''

"Harass you?'' He looked genuinely offended. "I'm sorry you regard my interest in you as annoying or threatening. I like you, Doc. Plain and simple. Stupid me, last night I figured the feeling was mutual.''

She hesitated, knowing the heat would hopelessly hit her face at any second. "I do like you, Nick. I couldn't deny that if I wanted to, but we're at different places in life. We want and need different things."

"For chrissakes, I didn't ask you to marry me." He pushed an agitated hand through his hair and focused on something outside the window, looking as steamed as she'd ever seen him.

"That would be rich." She laughed. "You...married. It boggles the mind." He gave her a sharp look. "The thing is, I don't know what you want from me. A little recreational sex maybe?"

Denial leaped into his eyes, and then guilt. "*Harmless, consensual,* recreational sex is more accurate."

"Explain that to me."

He made a sound of disgust. "What would you call last night's little tryst?"

"Hormones and poor judgment."

Incredibly, hurt flickered in his eyes. "Don't forget mutual."

"I haven't forgotten. Not in the least. And I'm not ignoring my responsibility—"

"Excuse me, Doc, but the way I see it, you're making an awfully big deal out of nothing."

She smiled sadly. "That's my point. Last night meant something to me. It was a big deal. If it happens again it could be an even bigger deal." The squeamish look on his face made her laugh. "Don't worry, I won't stalk you. I'm not *that* infatuated."

"Damn, I must be losing my touch." He chuckled but she could tell he was nervous.

"I'm getting off track. The main difference between us is that you're pretty much set on where you want to be in life. I'm still plodding along."

"I don't see your point." He saw something, judging by the way his jaw set and his eyes hardened.

"Put simply, you have a lot of time on your hands. I don't. I work two jobs and spend all my other waking time on my thesis. I don't have surplus energy to waste."

He sat silently, staring at her, his nostrils flaring, as though a lot was bubbling inside him, as though he were about to explode. Finally he said, "Maybe we should postpone the rest of this session."

If he was bluffing, he was in for a surprise. "I agree," she said, getting to her feet, exhaustion weighing heavily in her neck and shoulders. "About tomorrow's session..." She hesitated at his grim expression. "I'll call."

11

EVERYTHING HAD BACKFIRED on him.

Nick attacked the Chevy's hood with too much vigor. Hell, the thing didn't even need polishing. It already had a fresh coat from last week. With his recent luck, the Chevy would probably self-destruct from too much love and care.

Shit!

He thought he'd been so damn clever in passing off those raunchy letters as his dreams. Now Emma thought he was obsessed with sex. What crap! He didn't think about it any more than the average male. He liked sex. So what? He was a healthy twenty-nine-year-old, all parts in cherry condition. He was supposed to want sex, for God's sake. A body might even require it. Regular maintenance sure kept things tuned and lubed.

The phone rang, and he jumped to answer it. Midday already and he hadn't heard from Emma. Which couldn't be good news. She wasn't the type to keep him hanging. Although she didn't think he had anything else to do either.

The reminder stuck like a hard lump in his throat. Screw her. Maybe he shouldn't answer. Not that he'd have a choice since he couldn't find the damn phone. He rarely used the garage extension and had to stop and think a minute. It rang a third time and he followed the sound.

He tossed the heap of rags he'd brought from the dryer but it wasn't there. He kicked aside a stack of newspapers waiting to be recycled, sure the phone was behind them. No luck.

After the fourth ring, he located it in his wash bucket. Good thing the sucker was dry.

He clicked the button, started to say hello when he heard the dial tone. It had rung only four times. Three technically, since he'd gotten it on the fourth one. Who the hell hung up after three rings?

Emma would, of course, since unlike him, she had a busy schedule.

He cursed again.

Yeah, he'd been lucky most of his life, things had come easily and quickly. So what was he supposed to do? Give everything back? Deny his talent and ability to retain knowledge, or make money? Live the life of a monk in penance?

It wasn't as if he weren't grateful for the intellect he'd inherited, or the breaks that came his way. Hell, yeah, he was grateful. For all of it.

The phone rang again.

He still held it in his hand, but waited for the second ring before depressing the talk button.

"Nick?" Brenda's voice swamped him with disappointment.

"Yeah?"

"It's customary to say something when you answer a phone. You know, like hello, instead of just breathing heavy."

"And people generally let a phone ring more than three times."

"You picked it up on the second ring."

He sighed, perversely relieved. "You didn't call just a minute ago?"

"No. What's wrong?"

"Nothing. I'm just distracted."

Brenda snorted. "Must be contagious."

"What do you mean?" He had a feeling he knew just by the teasing note in his sister's voice.

"I talked to Emma earlier. She could barely keep two thoughts together."

"Oh, yeah?" He tried to sound casual when he wanted to demand to know everything they discussed. "She must be busy."

"No joke. She was at the restaurant right as the lunch crowd converged."

Disappointment hit him again. He wanted to be her distraction. "Where does she work, anyway?"

"Sorry. That's top secret."

He laughed.

"Really. She doesn't like people bothering her at work."

"She's supposed to call me about today's session." He glanced at his watch. "Which should start in three hours."

"If she said she'd call, she will."

He silently cleared his throat. "Did she say anything about it?"

"Nope. She never discusses you."

He wasn't sure how he felt about that anymore. "Admirable."

"What's your problem?"

Using the heel of his hand, he rubbed his eyes. One good night's sleep was all he needed. Or a romp with Emma. Damn! Maybe she was right. He was obsessed with sex...or at least obsessed with her. Man, he could not go there. "What did you call for?"

"Damn grouch, you made me forget." She paused, and made a clicking sound with her tongue. "Oh, yeah, Mom was sorry she didn't get to see more of you the other night and she wants you to go over for dinner this weekend."

"So now you're the messenger?"

"No, you turkey. She's going to call you later. I thought I'd give you a heads up."

Great. Everyone in Chapel Hill was calling him today but Emma. And now his mother wanted another shot at him and bachelorhood.

"Thanks," he muttered. "I'll be sure to let the answering machine pick up."

"Nick." That scolding tone always annoyed him. "If I have to go make nice, so do you."

"I was kidding. I'll go see her." *Eventually.* He glanced at his watch. "Look, I gotta go."

"One more question..."

"Shoot."

"Would it be uncomfortable for you if I asked Emma to dinner, too?"

EMMA STARED AT THE PHONE, confused, unnerved, wary, but it wasn't as if she had any choice. Nick was her last hope of completing her thesis in time. Surely he'd cooled off by now. In more ways than one.

Too bad she hadn't.

Maybe she should have sex with him. Or at least

accept the fact that she would once this study was completed. If it was all settled in her mind that she would, maybe she could get on with business instead of dwelling on "what if."

She was far more upset with herself than she was with him. For the first time in years, she couldn't stay focused. All she thought about was him. And sex. And what his skin and muscle would feel like beneath her palms. What it would feel like to have him buried deep inside her.

God help her, this wasn't like her at all.

With precious little time to fit everything in she had to do each day, she could ill afford this horrible, debilitating obsession.

She started to reach for the phone again, but immediately drew back. Her hands trembled and she was afraid her voice would do the same. It was frightening to think she could revert to old ways when she had to struggle to concentrate on every word, every sentence put before her.

How her mother would sneer about how her time and energy had been wasted, trying to help Emma behave and read like a normal child. The thought made her shudder.

But ironically, it also gave her strength. She reached for the phone, and dialed the number she now knew by heart. The line was busy.

She waited a minute, sank back onto her bed and idly petted Jake, while reminding herself she was a professional, and then tried again.

Still busy.

Okay, she was a firm believer that everything happened for a reason. She obviously needed a little more time to decide how she'd handle Nick. How she'd justify sleeping with him.

No, no, no. That's not what she was supposed to be thinking about. She backed away from the phone as if it were a rattlesnake that could strike at any time. Maybe she should just work off his notes. If she had any questions, she could e-mail him.

She shook her head. What a laugh he'd get over that suggestion after her high and mighty claim that she was a professional.

Jake let out a loud meow, and she looked at the digital clock. It wasn't feeding time yet. But time was running out to call Nick for today's session.

The cat whined again.

"Hey, you, what's the matter?" She scratched behind his ears in just the right spot. But that didn't seem to make him happy. "Ah, Jake, come here."

She tried to cuddle him but he jumped off the bed and gave her the tail. She didn't blame him for being mad at her. He hadn't received much attention in the past two days. She was too busy replaying conversations with Nick, and projecting various outcomes. None of them made her happy, and Jake had clearly picked up the bad vibes.

What the hell happened to her perfectly ordered life? Until Nick Ryder, no matter how busy or overwhelmed she was everything ran like clockwork.

She reached for the phone, but then stopped. Seeing him wasn't a good idea. Her emotions were too close to the surface. So how effective would she be, anyway?

Nick certainly wouldn't care if they met today. She doubted he cared much about anything.

She caught a glimpse of Jake prancing past her bedroom door without even so much as glancing her way.

Damn that Nick. Now even her cat was pissed at her.

THE PHONE RANG AGAIN. This made the fifth time this morning. First the hang-up call, and then Brenda, then someone who wanted to change his long distance service, and finally his mother. If this next caller was anyone but Emma, Nick was going to change his number. Make it unlisted. No one would have it. No exceptions.

Hell, he should've gotten caller ID like Brenda suggested. But to his thinking, either he felt like talking or he didn't, and knowing who was on the other end wouldn't change that. But then he hadn't known Emma.

Dammit.

"Hello?" It came out a growl.

"Geez, what the hell is your problem?"

He recognized Marshall's voice. "I thought you were someone else."

"Glad I'm not." He paused, and Nick could hear him take a drag off his cigarette. "Maybe this isn't a good time to ask if you have a few minutes."

"Looks like I'm going to have a few hours."

"Come again."

"Nothing." Nick sighed and massaged the tension at the back of his neck. "How are Sally and the kids?"

Marshall hesitated long enough to make Nick nervous. "They're fine."

"You sure?"

"Of course."

"Are *you* okay?"

"Remember in our junior year when you got sacked by Peter Munoz in the last quarter of our second game? You said it felt like being run over by a five-ton elephant. You were out of commission for two weeks, no football, no nothing."

"Remember? Hell, I think I still have the bruises." Marshall took another drag and then exhaled. "That's how I feel."

"Quit smoking. That should eliminate half your problems." Nick remembered the cigarette he'd smoked the other night just because he was pissed off, and he cringed.

"I wish it were that simple."

Nick frowned. Usually Marshall took a shot at Nick's vices, or told him to mind his own damn business. "What's wrong?"

"This is hard for me to ask."

"For God's sake, how long have we known each other?"

"Too long, you pain in the ass."

"That's what I was thinking." They both laughed, but Nick didn't like the sound of despair in his friend's voice.

"I need to borrow some money."

Relieved, Nick exhaled. "Give me a figure and I'll write the check."

"Sally can't know about this."

"It's strictly between us."

"I'll pay you back with my next bonus."

"No rush." He wondered if Marshall would tell

him what this was about. It didn't matter, except that Nick could offer more than financial support. "In fact, you don't need to. Consider it a gift."

"You don't even know how much I'm asking for."

"It's enough that you asked," Nick said quietly. "If you need anything else, you know I'm here for you."

Marshall laughed, the sound an odd mixture of bitterness and gratitude. "I knew I could count on you. Good ole Nick. You'd never find yourself in this situation."

A lick of anger flamed in Nick's gut. His friend was obviously in pain so Nick let go of the subtle reference to his so-called charmed life. "You want to tell me what this is about?"

"Nope. I've humbled myself enough for one day."

"Shit, Marsh, you're talking to me. We're friends. We're there for each other. Don't give me this humble crap."

"Yeah, I know. But this time I'll take a pass on giving an explanation."

"Your call." Nick glanced at his watch. Maybe he'd break down and phone Emma. "You want to pick up the check or should I drop it off?"

"You'll be home this evening?"

"Call first." Hell, maybe he'd still get lucky and see Emma. "Otherwise I can leave it under the mat."

"Thanks, Nick, I—thanks."

"You gonna tell me how much, or did you expect a blank check?"

Marshall laughed. He sounded a little better. After he gave Nick the amount, he said, "I have the money, but it's invested and Sally's signature is required before I can liquidate. It's not like I'm in financial trouble. I will pay you back."

"I'm not worried."

"I know." Marshall sighed. "Hell, pal, what I wouldn't give to be in your shoes. Footloose and fancy free."

"Yeah, what a life."

They hung up, and Nick stared at the Chevy, wondering what kind of trouble his friend was in. He wasn't curious by nature and generally he'd rather not know about his friend's personal business. But Marshall had always been the most rock-solid of all Nick's friends, knowing exactly what he wanted out of life, where he wanted to be, even as early as their college days.

Not only was he already at the top of his profession at a young age, he was the quintessential family man who adored his wife and kids. The idea that he was in any kind of trouble was damn disturbing.

Worrying about Marshall was almost enough to make Nick forget about Emma...until the phone rang again. He'd left the receiver next to him but let it ring a second time while he got an oath out of his system.

He knew it wasn't her. He'd given up on seeing her today. Probably shouldn't even answer. If it was a solicitor, Nick would likely rip the poor sap a new one. It had turned into just that kind of day.

He caved in and picked up the phone. "Yeah?"

"Nick?"

"Emma?"

"I hope I'm not disturbing you."

The mere sound of her voice made his heart thud. "Nah, I was just polishing the Chevy."

"Oh."

"But I could grab a shower and be over in forty minutes."

"That isn't necessary. I have a few questions about yesterday's session, but we can do it over the phone."

"Sure." Disappointment pricked him like a thorn.

"It should take only about ten minutes. Are you ready, or should I call back in a few?"

"Now's fine." He sank onto a large trash bag filled with leaves that should have gone to the curb this morning, and got comfortable.

"Okay, well most of the questions are the usual, like whether—"

"Doc?"

"Yes?" She sounded hesitant. No improvement over the strain in her voice.

"Are we okay?"

"I'm not sure I—if you mean—of course. Business as usual."

Right. "I gotta tell you, Doc. I didn't like the way we left things yesterday."

"Me neither." Her voice was soft, tentative. It cut through him like a switchblade.

He wondered what she'd say if he told her he'd dreamt of her again last night. "We're adults. We can put this disagreement behind us."

"At least one of us is."

He grinned. The old Doc was back. "I'm not even gonna ask."

She laughed. "Are you ready?"

Her rush back to business made his smile fade. "Go for it."

"First, did you know anyone in the dream?"

His mind went blank. "Refresh my memory, Doc. I'm not sure which dream we're talking about."

"The party by the lake."

"Party by the lake," he repeated, trying to recall which story that was. "Nope, I'm not recalling. What else?"

"Um...the two women?"

"Doc, all my dreams have women."

Her soft, plaintive sigh came across loud and clear, and he grinned. "Don't you have notes?" she asked.

"I left them with you, remember?"

"This isn't good. If you can't recall the dream, you certainly aren't going to remember the emotions or feelings that were evoked."

"Not necessarily. Give me a few more hints." He sank against the wall as the story came back in a sudden rush of clarity and excitement. The thought of hearing her retell it made his blood simmer.

"Well, you were at a lake with some friends, having a party when one of the women decided to go skinny-dipping. Ringing any bells?"

"Sort of. What else?"

"Another woman took off her clothes, too. Oh, and she had nipple rings." She paused as if she expected him to suddenly remember.

"And?"

"Doesn't that help?"

"Lots of women have nipple rings."

Silence.

He could guess how she'd interpreted that remark and it might've been funny if he wasn't getting hard, his skin prickly with arousal. "Look," he said matter-of-factly, "isn't there a defining situation that would jog my memory?"

She softly cleared her throat. "The women started making love, and then one of them called you over to go down on her." She paused. "You're messing with me, aren't you?"

"She wanted me to use my tongue and mouth?"

He heard her breath catch. "Yes."

"Make her wet and hot."

"Yes." Her voice was barely above a whisper.

"Spread her lips and find that one sensitive spot that would drive her wild?"

She groaned softly, and he closed his eyes and cupped the hardness beneath his fly, unsure who was suffering more.

"Did she want me to put my finger in her, and then make her come with my tongue?"

"Nick, you can't do this—" She panted his name, and the image of her on the other end, pleasuring herself had him unzipping his jeans.

"Am I getting it right, Emma?"

"Damn you." Her voice was as hoarse and raspy as his.

It took him a minute before he could speak again while she did nothing to break the silence. "Emma?"

Her breath shuddered into the phone. "I think it's time I had a look at your Chevy."

12

BRENDA SKIPPED HELLO. "Mom wants to have dinner tonight instead of waiting for the weekend."

Nick knew he shouldn't have picked up the phone, except he'd hoped it was Emma calling back to confirm a time she could come over. "Sorry, I'm busy."

"No, you aren't."

"How do you know?" He was still recovering from Emma's call a half hour ago, or he would've come up with a more notable remark.

"Because I just talked to Emma."

That got his attention. He threw the kitchen towel aside, closed the dishwasher door and picked up the beer he hadn't had time to open yet. The place didn't look too bad. It just needed a little picking up before she got there. "And?"

"And what?"

"Don't be a smart-ass."

Brenda snorted. "If I understood her correctly, which there is a distinct possibility I didn't since she was only semicoherent, you guys aren't meeting today."

"Semicoherent?" Dangerous ground, he knew, but his damned ego had a mind of its own.

"She said she'd just gotten up from a nap."

He smiled, and popped open the beer. "What else did she say?"

"Sorry, I think I've got the wrong number. I thought this was my brother Nick who normally isn't so nosy."

He grunted. Now Doc had him sounding like a lovesick teenager. "You know what I mean."

Brenda stayed silent for a long uncomfortable moment. "Nick, you aren't putting the moves on her, are you?"

"Right."

"I told you she was off-limits."

"Not that you have a say in my love life, but I understand Doc is different." He was going straight to hell. No doubt about it.

"Too evasive. Are you sleeping with her?"

"No." *Not yet.* "Not that it's any of your business. Look, I've got to go."

"What about tonight?"

"I told you I'm busy." He glanced at the clock, took a sip of beer. Emma could be trying to call back already. "Give Mom my regrets."

"I wish you'd reconsider. It would mean a lot to her."

Guilt nudged him. "Tell her I'll take her to dinner this weekend. There's a new sushi bar that opened near Duke Medical Center."

"Yeah, she'll love that." Brenda made a gagging sound. "If you change your mind, dinner is at seven-thirty." She paused. "Emma and I are getting there around seven."

"What?" Nick set down his beer. "Why is Emma going?"

"Because she was invited?"

His sister's sarcasm annoyed him at the best of times. He exhaled slowly. "When did—" This was unbelievable. What kind of game was Emma playing? "You just talked to her and she said she'd go."

"Not more than five minutes ago. Why?"

He cleared his throat. "She had some questions on yesterday's session, and she was going to call later. I guess I misunderstood."

"Well, you guys could get that out of the way after dinner."

What the hell was going on? Had Emma reconsidered and she was too chicken to tell him? Why would she go to his mom's for dinner? "Emma's never gone to dinner there with you before, has she?"

"I've asked her, but this time I'm not taking no for an answer. She's either working too hard, or running back to Utah to console her whining mother, which puts her further behind and she ends up working twice as hard."

"Her mom's ill?"

"Sick in the head, if you ask me. Shit! Don't tell Emma I said anything about her mother. Sore subject."

He wanted to know more, but he wouldn't get the information from Brenda. One thing about her, she respected a person's privacy and kept her mouth shut. He admired that, and normally wouldn't be so curious. Hell, it was more than curiosity. He wanted to understand Emma, know what made her tick.

He took another pull of beer, wondering what the devil Emma had been thinking when she'd accepted

Brenda's invitation. Maybe she'd been taken by surprise, or too incoherent as Brenda said.

"Hey, did you fall asleep on me?"

Nick sighed. Dammit, this wasn't what he had planned for tonight. "What time did you say dinner is?"

BRENDA HUNG UP the phone, and stared idly out her apartment window at the leaves that had started to turn orange. This was the perfect idea. Being able to observe them over dinner was more like it. The other night at the reception had been a waste. She was never able to see them interact.

She grinned. No, not a waste, really. The pot had obviously been stirred up some. They were both getting a little touchy when the other's name was mentioned. Something was definitely going on.

She leaned back and swung her feet onto her desk just like she'd asked Nick a dozen times not to do. No doubt they'd both be pissed at her when they found out she'd lied. Emma hadn't agreed to go tonight until she found out Nick would be there. Which, of course, he hadn't...yet.

Brenda smiled. That's okay. She could take whatever either of them dished out. It was all for a good cause.

THE SOUTHERN PLANTATION-STYLE HOUSE was an awesome sight. Huge and pristine white with ivy crawling up two of the pillars at the far ends of the porch. The velvety green lawn stretched over several gentle slopes headed toward a greenbelt on the left. To the right was a large greenhouse. A staggering procession of vibrant scarlet mums lined the curved driveway Brenda navigated with a tad too much speed.

Emma knew the Ryder family had money, but the neighborhood and the house were still a little overwhelming. Her family home outside of Provo was a modest three-bedroom tract home. Before that, until she was nine, they'd lived in a trailer park.

"I hope we'll eat outside by the pool since it's not too cool yet," Brenda said, ignoring the cluster of mums she nearly sideswiped as she pulled the car into the circular part of the drive directly in front of the house.

They were running late, yet there were no other cars on the drive. Nick was supposed to be here. Which Emma still didn't understand. Had he reconsidered having her over to his place and was too chicken to tell her? That didn't sound like him. Maybe Brenda had caught him off guard like she had Emma, or maybe...

"Are you going to get out or sit there daydreaming?" Brenda had already come around the hood of the car and opened the passenger door.

Her sometimes caustic grin had never bothered Emma before, but it sure grated on her nerves now. As she got out, a sudden suspicion seeded, and she squinted at Brenda. Was this all a ploy to keep them apart? How many times had she warned Emma about Nick, had told her to not get involved with him?

That was silly. She wouldn't have known that Emma had made a fool of herself by practically inviting herself over to Nick's place. The reminder of their conversation heated her face and took some spring out of her step, and she almost finished off the mums Brenda narrowly missed.

"I think we're having gumbo and shrimp étouffée. It won't be too spicy so don't worry." Brenda continued chattering all the way to the front door, where she stopped to ring the bell, but then opened the door herself and went in. "Cookie's from New Orleans and she's the best cook Mom ever had, even though she is rather bossy."

"I heard that." A woman appeared out of nowhere, short and painfully thin, the apron she wore nearly wrapped around her fragile waist twice.

"Hi, Cookie." Brenda gave the woman a hug and lifted her off the ground. "It smells good in here."

The woman swatted Brenda with the wooden spoon she carried. "I don't know why y'all ring the bell and then let yourselves in. Why can't you and that rascal brother of yours do one or the other? Instead of makin' me walk all the way from the kitchen." The gruff affection in her voice made Emma smile. "Where is that scoundrel, anyway? It's been too long since he's come home for some of Cookie's cookin'."

"He'll be along any minute," Brenda said, and then turned to Emma. "Meet my friend Emma Snow."

Cookie ducked her head to see past Brenda, her eyes lighting with interest when they met Emma's. "Well, I guess he will be right along, like a stallion to water." She extended a bony, blue-veined hand. "Very nice to meet you, Emma Snow."

She had a firm grip for such a little thing, who was probably pushing sixty, although it was hard to tell with that mop of unnatural black hair.

"Same here. Now, I'm going to ask the same thing I'm sure everyone else does. Is Cookie your real name?"

"Lord, yes, why would I inflict that upon myself?" The woman chuckled and waved them to follow her. "My mama was not the sharpest tool in the shed, but she had a sense of humor, bless her heart. I hope y'all are hungry."

Not the answer Emma had expected but she smiled at Cookie's charming Southern accent. Even though North Carolina was considered the south, the medical center and universities in Chapel Hill and Durham drew an extensive hodgepodge of immigrants from other states and countries and a true Southerner was seldom heard.

Brenda sidled up and whispered, "That's how she chose her profession. Because of her name. Isn't she a kick?"

"No whisperin' in this house, missy," Cookie called without looking back. "Mind your manners."

"Yes, ma'am." Brenda grinned and whispered something else, but the doorbell chimes drowned it out.

Cookie had just entered the kitchen but she made an about-face and hurried past them toward the door, which was already opening. "You see what I mean? That rascal."

Her fondness for Nick was plain, even before she rushed him with a bear hug and a good-natured scolding. He swept her up in his arms and twirled her around, mindless of the large bouquet of flowers he'd brought.

He set her down and gave her a long serious look.

"How come you're gettin' prettier and younger every day?" he asked, and she smacked his arm. "Now, darlin' I don't understand it. You explain it to me."

Emma was amazed at how Southern he sounded, but she wasn't the least surprised at how she responded to him. Her skin had grown warm and her belly and nipples tight. Maybe coming tonight wasn't such a good idea. Hugging herself, she moved back near the circular staircase, and out of view.

"You're a rascal and a scoundrel," Cookie said, waving the wooden spoon. "Always have been, always will be."

"Yes, ma'am." He grinned and handed her the flowers.

"You give them to your mama yourself when she comes down from gettin' ready. Lord knows you neglect her enough."

He ducked his head and kissed Cookie's cheek. "But these are for you darlin'. Now, where's that rotten sister of mine?" Brenda had disappeared into the kitchen but she came out licking her fingers.

Cookie looked up from the flowers she was sniffing and glared. "Git out of my kitchen."

"The étouffée is primo," Brenda said, making a circular sign with her thumb and forefinger.

"Doggone it." Cookie raised her wooden spoon and headed toward Brenda, who turned and scrambled in the other direction.

The two women disappeared and Emma turned back toward Nick. He was looking straight at her, his dark eyes intense, unreadable. She stepped out from beneath the staircase feeling foolish. He'd probably seen her all along.

"Hey," she said lamely.

He made a movement with his head, acknowledging her. "You just get here?"

"Yeah." She shrugged, hating the sudden awkwardness between them. "A few minutes ago."

"My mother hasn't come down yet?"

Emma shook her head. "I haven't seen her."

"She likes making an entrance." Slowly, he moved toward Emma. "I'd say she'll be another ten minutes."

He got close, too close, and when Emma tried to back up, she realized she was up against the wall with no place to go. Her mouth went dry and her head got a little light.

He stepped closer.

Her stomach somersaulted. She was being silly. He wouldn't do anything here.

"I grew up in this house," he said, his voice lowering as he got closer still. "I know every creak in the floorboard and the stairs. No one could sneak up on me."

"Oh." She swallowed when he reached out and fingered a long renegade tendril of hair. She'd left it down but had stubbornly worn her glasses.

"Come here." He trailed his hand down her arm until their palms met, and then he circled his fingers around her wrist and gave her a small tug toward him.

"Nick." She cast a nervous glance around. They were definitely alone behind the staircase. From the kitchen, she could hear Brenda's laughter, Cookie's grumbling.

She turned back to him and without warning he pressed her back against the wall, covering her mouth with his, and parting her lips with his tongue. She whimpered in protest, or maybe surrender. When she tried to draw her head back, the wall stopped her.

He pressed harder until she felt his arousal, hot and heavy, through her khaki slacks and thin cotton sweater. Her breath caught and his tongue dove deeper. Helplessly she started to respond when a noise came from the top of the stairs.

Nick was quick to pull away, but then he came back for a brief, parting kiss before he put a respectable distance between them.

"That's got to be Mother." He straightened Emma's glasses and winked. "I smell her perfume."

She swatted his hand away and adjusted her glasses to her own liking. "Excuse me," she said, trying to push past him and get out from under the stairs.

He moved aside and with a sweep of his hand, motioned for her to pass. As soon as she stepped out into the foyer, Mrs. Ryder came around the curve of the stairs, her eyes widening, clearly startled by Emma's sudden appearance.

When Nick moved in to stand behind her, Mrs. Ryder pressed her lips together but couldn't quite conceal her smile. Emma didn't even try to keep her face from flaming. That would have been useless, but she sure would have a few choice words for Nick later.

"So good of you to come, Emma," Mrs. Ryder said, extending her hand as she left the stairs. Her fuchsia silk pantsuit set off her gorgeous, upswept blond hair. Even her perfectly manicured nails and lips were painted fuchsia—probably about the same color as Emma's face. "Brenda has told me a great deal about you."

For a second, Emma had the foolish hope that Mrs. Ryder didn't recognize her from the reception. But that might be asking too much. "Thanks for having me. It'll be nice to have something for dinner that hasn't already been frozen."

Mrs. Ryder shook her head. "The way you college kids eat..." She looked at Nick with a blank expression. "Well, Emma, who's your friend?"

Emma blinked. The woman was too young to be senile.

He groaned. "Knock it off, Mom, you just saw me the other night."

Mrs. Ryder's arched brow wrinkled. "No, you don't look familiar at all. Of course I once had a son who looked like you but since he never comes around..."

He kissed her cheek as she lifted her chin in defiance. "Very funny, but if you don't knock it off, I'll have to give your present to someone else."

Her gaze flew to Nick's empty hands.

He chuckled. "I thought that might interest you. It's in the car."

"Hmm, so it must be bigger than a breadbox." The older woman gave Emma a probing look. "Do you know what it is?"

"Not a clue." Emma smiled at the interchange between mother and son. Their fondness for each other was palpable and it made Emma envious and wistful.

"You don't get it until after you feed me." Nick put an arm around his mother, and then shocked Emma by putting his other one around her. "Now,

what say we go into the kitchen and bug Cookie for
some hors d'oeuvres.''

Emma relaxed fairly quickly under his comfortable,
non-threatening touch. It was kind of nice, actually,
to be included in this familiar sort of way, and since
his mother had no reaction, Emma didn't balk. She
let him guide them through the formal dining room
with the sparkling crystal display, gleaming hardwood
floors and Persian rug to the kitchen.

The room was enormous, full of bright sunlight,
green plants, polished brass and heady aromas. The
setup was a cook's dream—state-of-the-art appli-
ances, a large tiled island with an additional sink and
enough cupboard space to house Emma's entire apartment.

Brenda looked up from the pot she was stirring, her
mouth obviously full of something. She chewed
quickly, swallowed. ''Where have you guys been?
I've practically eaten dinner single-handedly.''

''You better not have, missy.'' Carrying a bag of
sugar, Cookie came through a door off to the side,
apparently the pantry. ''You kids must be eatin'
nothin' but junk the way you come swooping in here
like vultures.''

''Not me,'' Nick said, letting the women go and
diving for a deviled egg off a silver tray.

They all laughed.

Cookie set down the sugar and swatted him with a
dish towel. ''Make yourself useful and get out that
other tray of cut vegetables from the fridge.''

Nick made a face. ''Nah, we don't need that.''

''Git.'' Cookie snapped the towel. ''And make
your guest something to drink.''

"Yes, ma'am." He winked at Cookie and then turned and gave Emma a sultry look that made her knees weak.

She didn't know how he did it. The way he could laugh and joke one minute, and then shoot her a look that said he wanted to climb inside her until she screamed. It was both annoying and exciting, and terribly disconcerting in the presence of his family. Bad enough, on the way over, Brenda had given her yet another lecture on not getting involved with Nick.

Without asking, he made Emma a mint julep, strong enough that she felt a slight buzz by the time they sat down to dinner in the patio by the pool. She liked it a lot that Cookie sat with them after she and Brenda served the food. The cook was treated as if she were family and it made Emma like the entire Ryder clan even more, if that were at all possible.

If anyone noticed that Nick rather purposely sat beside her they didn't comment. And if they had the slightest suspicion that he touched her thigh every chance he got, they didn't react to that either. But he was rather sly about it and if anything gave them away it would be her pink cheeks.

The fact that he'd chosen tonight of all nights to accept his mother's dinner invitation still disturbed Emma. At least it was obvious it hadn't been an excuse to get away from her.

"Tell me, Emma, what do you plan to do after you get your master's?" Mrs. Ryder asked after carefully dabbing her mouth with the white linen napkin. She'd passed up Cookie's pecan pie and sipped coffee while everyone else gorged on the incredibly sweet and wonderful treat.

Emma dutifully swallowed before answering. "I have a job lined up at a clinic in Raleigh."

"That's quite impressive to have that kind of security while you're still studying. They obviously think very highly of you."

Emma winced. "They'll think far more of my degree. Once I have it in hand, they'll assimilate me into the staff."

"Ah, yes, Brenda said you're working on your thesis." She glanced at Nick. "And you've offered to help by being her test subject, I understand. I'm very proud of you, Nicky."

He shifted, looking uncomfortable. "I didn't exactly volunteer. My dear sister twisted my arm."

Brenda laughed. "I did more than that. Anybody want this last piece of pecan pie?"

Cookie grabbed the glass pie plate out from under Brenda's reaching hand. "You've had enough, missy. I won't be letting out any more of your clothes."

"Cookie! That was rude." Brenda turned several shades of pink, and Emma felt for her, especially knowing that her friend was touchy about the last five pounds she'd put on.

"The truth is never rude." Sniffing, the older woman carried the remaining pie to the counter.

"Now, I believe Bren's right," Nick said, a glimmer of anger in his eyes as he purposefully snagged Cookie's gaze. "That was rude, even though you were kidding."

Cookie scowled and darted a look at Brenda who stared down at her napkin and had missed the interchange. She really was hurt, and Nick had been quick to defend her. Emma wanted to jump up and hug him.

"Lord, she knows I'm kiddin'." Cookie brought the piece of pecan pie back to the table. "Don't you, honey?"

Brenda shrugged and pushed the pie plate away. "It doesn't matter. You're right."

Mrs. Ryder cleared her throat, and then deftly changed the subject. "Emma, I'm interested in this clinic where you'll be working. Would I know the place?"

"I don't know. It's rather small and dependent upon federal and private donations. They mostly treat children from underprivileged families who couldn't afford therapy otherwise."

Emma felt Nick staring at her and she carefully avoided his eyes. Did he think it was a waste for her to work in a place that could never afford to pay her a high salary? Her mother had pointed that out more than once, until Emma had uncharacteristically but forcefully told her the subject was closed.

"That's marvelous." Mrs. Ryder set aside her coffee. "Isn't it, Nick?"

Emma was forced to glance his way, and the pride and admiration in his eyes made her heart skip a couple of beats. She reached for her water and took an embarrassingly noisy gulp.

"Yup, Doc is full of surprises." He smiled at her, a very intimate smile that sent a shiver of anticipation down her spine.

"I think it's particularly commendable that you work with children." Mrs. Ryder straightened as she warmed to the subject. "I strongly believe that most of our society's ills stem from poor family values."

Out of the corner of her eye, Emma caught Brenda and Nick exchanging wary glances.

"Tell me, Emma," Mrs. Ryder said, smiling, inclining her head, and Emma realized where Nick got his indefinable charm. "Are you planning on having children of your own?"

Emma blinked. Her thoughts scattered. "Well—"

"Don't start, Mom." Nick gave her a warning look.

Brenda sighed.

Cookie had been going back and forth, carrying dishes to the kitchen. She shook her head in disgust as she removed the last of the dessert plates. "Oh, Lord, here it comes."

"Pardon me, but can't I make a little polite conversation without you all acting like a bunch of—" Mrs. Ryder's brows lifted in indignation, and then so did her chin. "I will not reduce myself to your level."

"Good." Nick stood and gathered up the linen napkins. "Emma, you want a ride home?"

"You're not leaving yet." Mrs. Ryder stared incredulously at her son.

"Mom, once again you managed to make dinner last three hours. It's after ten o'clock. Yes, I'm going home."

Mrs. Ryder continued to plead her case, but it was difficult for Emma to register exactly what was going on. All she could think about was riding home with Nick. Would he take her straight home? Or would he suggest they go to his house? Would Brenda—

Brenda!

Emma had almost forgotten. Her gaze flew to her

friend. Brenda stared back with curiosity in her eyes, a curve of amusement to her lips.

She leaned close and whispered, "Go ahead. Ride home with Nick while I help Cookie clean up. But remember, you don't want to get involved with someone like him."

13

"WHAT WAS BRENDA'S BIG SECRET?"

Emma didn't like playing dumb, but... "What secret?"

"At the table after I asked if you wanted a ride. You two went into a huddle." Nick hadn't asked her yet whether she wanted to go to his place or home. The direction they were headed meant either one. "I have a good idea what it was. She warned you to stay away from me."

His voice revealed nothing so Emma gave him a sideways glance. The Porsche's top was down and there was plenty of light from the streetlamps. He seemed unfazed.

"She said the same to me."

Emma swung her head around to look directly at him. The wind whipped her hair about her face. She caught it in her fist. "She warned you about me?"

"Yep."

Suspicious, she squinted at him. "When?"

"While you were saying good-night to my mom and Cookie."

She had seen Brenda talking to him. But why warn Nick? Emma was relatively harmless— She laughed when she realized he was teasing her. "She warned *you* to stay away from me."

He smiled and glanced at her before returning his attention to the road. "Isn't that what I said?"

She took a deep breath. "Should I be worried, Nick? Should I listen to Brenda?"

His smile vanished. "You want an objective answer? Ask someone else."

"I'm sorry. I guess I'm just a little nervous."

He rotated a shoulder. "I won't force you to do anything you don't want to do, Doc. At the next light, we either go right to my place, or left to drop you at home." He paused and she stared with fascinated interest at the way his jaw flexed. She hadn't seen that before. "The Chevy is polished and tuned waiting to give you a ride. It's your choice."

It helped that he was obviously off balance, too. But only a little. If she had half a brain in her head, she would put off any decision until after the study was complete. Easier said than done. She hadn't been able to concentrate the past two days. On anything.

"Tell me something first." She turned in her seat to really study him. His hair needed trimming and the wind was doing a number on it. The crow's feet that crinkled at the corner of his eye as he squinted against the wind only made him look more attractive, slightly rugged, as did the summer tan that lingered. "About tonight. When I talked to you earlier, you already knew you were going to your mom's—"

"No, I didn't." He shot her a curious look. "I only accepted after Brenda told me you two were going."

Emma sighed. "What a buttinski."

"She played us." He snorted. "A lump of coal this Christmas for sure."

"But how did she know we had plans tonight?"

"How did she know Shannon Swanson was the first girl I kissed?"

"Excuse me?"

Nick chuckled. "My sister is quite resourceful when it comes to digging up information."

She grinned, thinking of a teenage Nick. "How old were you when you kissed Shannon?"

"Like I can remember that far back?" He slowed the car. "Well, Emma, it seems we've come to the next red light."

He turned to her, the desire in his eyes burning a hole straight through her good sense. She swallowed, and then said, "I'd really like to see your Chevy."

NICK LEANED against his work counter and watched Emma circle the Chevy. The appreciation in her gaze, the way she reverently touched the chrome, sent an odd sensation through his entire body. She understood the reason for the time and sweat he'd poured into the classic. And he hadn't had to say a word.

"Want me to put the top down?" He pushed off the counter.

"If you wouldn't mind?"

"There is a small charge."

She turned abruptly toward him, a question in her eyes.

He caught her around the waist and pulled her in close. "One kiss will do it."

Her mouth curved in such a slow sensual smile he had some serious reaction below the belt. When their lips touched, he knew he was in deep trouble. He took a small taste and then pulled away.

She seemed confused, maybe even a little hurt, so

he dove back in for some reassurance, but then disengaged before the fireworks started too soon.

"If you grab one side we'll get it down quicker," he said as he headed around the car. "I'll tell you what to do."

"I know how to do it."

He handled his end but kept an eye on how deftly she lowered and then secured the canvas Carson top.

"Hey, quit loafing on your side." She stood with her hands on her hips, waiting for him to finish.

"Yes, ma'am." He stepped back to admire the car, to admire Emma. "You want to go for a spin?"

"I thought you'd never ask." A seductively shy smile curved her lips.

Their gazes held and blood rushed to his groin when he realized they were talking about more than the Chevy. At least that was his hope.

"Hop in." He yanked his keys out of his pocket, anxious for the ride to be over.

After circling the block, he asked, "Tell me about that neighbor of yours back in Utah...the one with the Chevy."

"Mr. Salisbury. He used to let me help him wash and polish it."

"How old were you?"

She wrinkled her nose. "About eleven, twelve. I went to his house every day after school until it was time for dinner or homework."

"Odd way for a girl that age to spend her time."

She got quiet for a minute. "Mr. Salisbury was a nice man, my best friend, really. He was patient with me."

Her tone, her reluctance, even her posture told him

there was much more to the story. "Any brothers and sisters?"

"Nope, just my mom and me until she married my stepfather."

"You get along with them?"

She turned her head and pretended to look at the scenery, only it was too dark. "I had a learning disorder as a child. My mother spent a lot of time working with me so that I could keep up in school. You have a nice neighborhood."

"Yeah." He got the message loud and clear. The subject was closed. But he wanted more.

After circling the second block, he pulled into his drive.

"That's it?" Emma asked, when they coasted back into the garage.

"Nope." He depressed the button for the garage door to go down and then patted the seat between them. "The view's pretty good from over here."

She laughed. "My, oh, my, you are a rascal." She mimicked Cookie's Southern accent to perfection, but that wasn't what interested him right now. "Surely you weren't thinkin' of neckin' in this fine piece of automobile."

"Surely I am." He patted the seat again.

"I don't know, Nick...."

"I don't bite. Anyway, I've had my rabies vaccine."

She smiled and moved a few inches closer, still leaving too much space between them, uncertainty and shyness in her eyes.

"Nothing's going to happen that you don't want to happen. I promise."

She moved a little closer.

"Come here." He slid his arm behind her and then waited for her to slip over another few inches before he tightened his hold.

She rested her head on his shoulder. "We should be outside looking at the stars."

"What? You don't like the way I decorated my garage?"

She laughed softly. "I understand stacks of newspaper and baskets of glass to be recycled are very chic accessories this season."

"But we're in a '55 Chevy."

"Silly me."

"Okay, so this isn't the most romantic place, but in a minute the garage light will go out and we won't have to worry about some cop shining his flashlight in our faces."

She faked a shiver. "There is certainly that."

"And then there's this." He lifted her chin and gently pressed his mouth to hers. She tensed but she didn't tell him to stop. "And this." He leisurely trailed his lips down the side of her neck, and she began to relax. "And this." He bit her earlobe, and then ran the tip of his tongue along the shell of her ear.

She drew back and he half expected a protest, but she took off her glasses and then touched his lips with hers, gently, hesitantly, but it was a start.

When she drew back again, she shook her head. "This isn't right. If the study were over—"

"The study is going just fine." He kissed her again, harder this time and he felt her start to thaw.

Surprising him, she splayed her hand across his

chest. She slipped a finger inside the front of his chambray shirt and found his hardened nipple.

Like an awkward teenaged boy, he fumbled for the buttons of her blouse. She kissed him harder, opening for his tongue while he managed to get three buttons unfastened.

Her bra was made of skimpy lace with a front closure. He guessed it was black, or maybe red. He wanted to see what he felt beneath his palm, how the soft mound of skin swelled over the lace cup. Just as he pulled back, the overhead light went out.

He bit back a curse.

"You're overdressed," she whispered as she slid his buttons from their holes.

He sat back, letting her finish before he tackled the remainder of hers. Her blouse slid easily off her shoulders and the bra hook disengaged with barely a touch.

"Let's turn on the light," he whispered as he nuzzled her neck and cupped the weight of her soft breasts in each of his hands.

"We have enough." She pushed forward, filling his palms, a soft whimpering sound coming from her throat, making him too hard, too soon.

Lowering his head, he greedily suckled her, gathering her breasts together so he could have both nipples at once. She thrust her chest forward, giving him his fill, while raking her hands through his hair and moaning softly.

Reluctantly he retreated, and then shrugged out of his shirt, anxious to feel her pearled nipples against his skin. He shifted and then leaned back, and she readily followed. Her skin was warm and soft and scented with vanilla. He inhaled the subtle fragrance while his hands roamed her back, forcing her closer so that not a breath of air separated them.

"Emma?"

She looked up from kissing the side of his neck, and a faint beam of moonlight coming through the window fell upon her full moist lips. Long strands of brown hair wound over her bare shoulders and clung to her damp skin. Did she even know how incredibly beautiful she was?

He lifted his head to capture her mouth and she came to him eagerly, meeting his tongue, diving deep as if she couldn't get enough of him. The mere idea fueled such a raging mindless desire, making him so hard he throbbed, and making him wonder which was bigger, his ego or his erection.

It was easy to slide his fingers beneath the waist of her khakis as he massaged the small of her back, but he could only go far enough to get a hint of the firm yet soft curves of flesh. He understood what a person going through withdrawal felt like as he reached between them to undo her zipper. It slid down easily, revealing more lace. A second later he found her wet heat.

She bucked slightly when he touched her, and then moaned when he slid a finger inside her slick folds. She was so wet and ready he had trouble catching his breath. That she again deepened the kiss nearly made him explode.

He withdrew, and then re-entered her with two fingers. She clenched her muscles around them and moved her hips, and he knew he wouldn't make it much longer.

"Take your pants off, Nick." Her voice was barely audible and so ragged he hoped he'd heard right.

But then she raised herself and sat back in confirmation.

God, how he wished there was enough light so he could see her. Although the outline of her curves and her flowing hair were enough to worry him. He'd never embarrassed himself with a woman before, but he was damn close.

Apparently growing impatient, she attacked his zipper with anxious fingers that did nothing to help his threatening condition. He gently took over the task but found his jeans weren't going far. Cramped as they were, he only managed to shove them down a few inches.

He groaned. "Does this bring back old memories?"

"Huh?"

"We're going to have to do some shifting, sweetheart." What an idiot he'd been to start this out here when he had a nice, soft king-size bed inside.

"I don't understand." She leaned forward and he caught a sway of her breasts in the semidarkness.

"You're so damned beautiful." He touched her cheek, felt the heat rushing there.

She stiffened a little. "Nick," she whispered, sounding so sweet and tentative. "Tell me how to please you."

Her simple quiet statement took him by surprise. "You already please me. The sound of your voice, the intelligence in your eyes, your sense of humor, the color of your hair, your mouth...it all pleases me."

And scared the hell out of him because he'd never said anything like that to a woman before. Yet he meant every word because it felt right saying it to Emma.

"I'm serious, Nick." She laid her hand on his thigh. "It's not like I'm a virgin or anything, but I've only been with one other guy, and it—well, it hardly counted."

He hadn't really thought about how experienced she was, or wasn't. Not that it mattered. As long as she was comfortable with... He stiffened when her hand wandered up higher on his thigh and touched skin. He had to get them moved inside while he could still think. She didn't deserve to be laid out on the seat of a car. Not Emma.

His intention was cut short when her hand grasped his erection. He groaned. "You really don't understand. I can't—" He groaned again. "Emma, you can't do that."

Her grip tightened and then slackened. "Too much pressure? Tell me."

"No, it's not but—" He about left the seat when she completely circled her hand around him and stroked the base. "Wait! I'm gonna come in two seconds if you don't stop that."

He manacled her wrists with his fingers and forced her to stop. She moved so that her nipples rubbed the head, and he groaned. Caught off guard, he didn't see her lower her head until it was too late. She pursed her lips around him and took most of him into her mouth.

He had to...

He had to stop her before...

Oh, man.

"Emma." He shuddered, roughly pushing her away. More roughly than he'd intended.

Not that it bothered her. She closed her mouth around him again, and all the fantasies he'd had, picturing her full lips around his penis surged with the force of a tidal wave. How could he stop her when he wanted to come right now, right here in the Chevy?

Shit!

Not here. "Emma." He cupped her face and forced her chin up. Reluctantly she released him, and looked up, her eyes glazed and slightly wild in the moonlight. A sheen of moisture coated her pouting lower lip, hovering just inches above his slick, throbbing head.

He had to close his eyes against the image before he changed his mind and plunged into her right now.

"Nick?" The shyness in her voice did something funny to his heart. "What's wrong?"

He took two deep breaths. "Nothing." He took another. "I don't want to come too quickly."

"Is that all?"

"Yep." His breathing would never be normal again.

Mischief flashed in her grin before she started to lower her head again.

"Oh, no, you don't." He grabbed her wrists and raised himself to a sitting position.

Surprised, she fell back. Before she could straighten, he hunched over her.

"This is the way it's going to be, Emma." He reached again for her khakis. "In a minute we're going inside." He yanked them down as far as they would go. "Straight to my bedroom." He peeled down her lace panties, and she gasped. "You have a problem with that?"

"No," she whispered, lying perfectly still.

"You'll wait for me there while I get us a chilled bottle of wine." He had to do something to cool off. As if this helped, he thought as he kissed her smooth soft belly, and then lower.

He couldn't spread her thighs far enough but he managed to work his way between them, using the tip of his tongue until she moaned softly. Frustrated, he slid his hands under her firm warm bottom and lifted her to his mouth. Just one taste, that's all he wanted before they went inside.

Emma clutched the side of the seat. Sex had never been like this before. Wave after wave of new sensations washed over her body. Her skin was so sensitive, her nipples were so tight she thought she might explode at any moment.

She jumped when Nick pried her thighs apart, moaned when he spread her lips and nearly died when his tongue trailed the needy pearl of heat between them. Never had she let a man put his mouth there before, but this was Nick and…

"Oh, oh…" Her entire body tensed. Something was happening. She tried to squirm away. His fingers dug into her fleshy buttocks, holding her in place while he sucked and licked and drove her insane. "Nick, I thought we— Oh, Nick."

She shoved at his head, and ended up weaving her fingers through his hair. The greed with which he used his mouth was enough to push her over the edge and the explosion came immediately.

Low guttural noises echoed off the walls as her body coiled into a ball of fire, burning out of control, raging through her without mercy. She couldn't breathe, couldn't think. And then she went limp.

Nick wouldn't back off. He kissed and licked some more until she grabbed a handful of hair and tugged hard enough he brought his face up.

That didn't stop him. He kissed the top of her thighs, moved his mouth to her belly and then drew a nipple into his mouth and sucked until she started to feel the heat engulf her again.

"Nick, please, I want you inside me."

He brought his mouth to hers, covering it with urgency until she could taste his hunger and desperation and her own muskiness.

When he finally broke away, he drew back and stared at her. It was maddening not to be able to see his face. Faded as it was, all the light shone on her.

"Emma."

The reverent way he said her name made her shudder. "Nick, please."

He pushed the hair away from her damp cheek, placed a feather-light kiss on her eyelid. "We have to go inside. I don't have any protection out here."

"Oh." It sickened her to think she hadn't even considered that one monumental point. It sobered her a bit, too. But then when she went to sit up, his arousal lay hot and heavy against her belly and another wave of desire washed over her.

"You okay?" he asked, dragging the back of his knuckle down her cheek.

She nodded. "You?"

He chuckled. "Nope."

"What's wrong?" She'd never used her mouth like that before and maybe she... His sex throbbed against her, and she got it. What was wrong was that he hadn't gotten release yet.

"Go," she said, giving his chest a gentle push. "I'll meet you inside in a few minutes."

"No, come with me now." He kissed the back of her hand.

"I need a minute or two, and I'd bet you do, too."

"Why?"

"Were you expecting company?"

He stilled for a moment. "Yeah, you're probably right."

She smiled, thinking about her own room and the unmade bed and pile of clothes in the corner. Not company-ready. That's for sure.

"Two minutes, okay?" He kissed her hand again, and then her mouth. "Make that one."

"Go." She gave him a playful shove, wishing the lighting were better as she squinted into the semi-darkness and watched him pull up his pants and sling his shirt over his shoulder.

She started pulling herself together as he hopped out of the car.

"Come in through here," he said, pausing at a door at the top of a couple of steps. "It'll lead you into the kitchen."

"I'll be right there."

"You'd better," he said, his voice low and sexy and making her want to charge in right now.

She waited a few seconds after he'd disappeared before she got up, turned on a light, fumbled for her glasses and checked her face in the mirror. Flushed cheeks, smeared mascara, nothing unexpected, but her hair sure was a mess. She looked around for where she'd thrown her purse. It sat atop a stack of magazines.

She pulled out a brush and started the task of detangling her hair when the top magazine caught her attention. The cover was a picture of a half-naked woman, wrapped in red satin, sprawled across a love seat right below the name *Midnight Fantasy*.

Emma had heard of the publication but had never seen an issue. Curious, she picked it up and started leafing through the pages. Some of the pictorials made her shake her head but the cartoons made her laugh. When she got to the letters, she knew she wouldn't have time to read any but she was awfully curious. She quickly skimmed the first one, amazed at how graphic it was.

A paragraph into the second letter, she experienced an extraordinary sense of déjà vu. She read a few more lines. Maybe her head was still foggy but this...

It suddenly struck her why it sounded familiar. Her heart thudded. Her stomach rolled with disgust and disbelief. Nick wouldn't do that. He couldn't. He knew how important this study was to her.

Heart pounding, she continued reading. Finally, in abject despair she dropped the magazine and accepted the fact that she'd been royally screwed. She automatically wrapped her arms around herself, as though she could fend off the betrayal, protect her body from his violation.

How could he have done this? How could she have been so gullible? It was her own fault. Brenda had warned her not to get mixed up with Nick. Emma herself knew better than to dally on the wild side. The shame of it all was that she still didn't want to believe it.

She swallowed, hiccupped, sniffed. Without tending the rest of her hair, she stuck the brush back into her bag, and then carefully replaced the magazine on top of the stack. She'd just tucked in her blouse when she heard the door open.

"It's getting lonely in here." Nick stood in the doorway, shirtless and sexy, wearing the grin that used to make her head get light.

"I have to go," she said, wishing she had her own car. "Would you please take me home?"

His face darkened with confusion. "But—"

"Now, Nick." She turned away in case the tears started.

14

NICK SAT in the Porsche while Emma let herself into her apartment without so much as a backward glance. Long after she closed the door and the inside light came on, he sat there, shock rendering him motionless.

What the hell had happened? He'd left her alone for five minutes, six tops, and returned to find a totally different woman. She'd gone from soft and loving to tense and almost angry. That she'd given him the silent treatment all the way to her place didn't surprise him. He just wished he knew what had gone wrong.

Maybe she regretted the shift in their relationship. Her work was important to her and she was very much a professional. If only she'd said something, anything, he would have had the opportunity to convince her that nothing had changed.

He stared into the darkness. He just didn't get it. She'd gone from hot to cold so fast there had to be something more bothering her. Could he have been too forward and scared her?

Could she be embarrassed now?

Speculating was pointless. It only made him crazy. He started the car and jammed it into gear. As much as he'd wanted to have her in his bed tonight, his biggest regret was that he hadn't confessed to the juvenile stunt he'd pulled by using the magazine stories.

At dinner he'd pretty much decided it was time to cut the crap. Hearing her speak passionately of the clinic where she'd be working, and seeing the joy in her eyes had really gotten him thinking. With the bogus information he'd fed her, the study would be tainted. Thank God he'd kept notes of his real dreams, the dreams where she'd taken center stage.

He wasn't stupid enough to think she'd take his confession lightly. But he figured it would've gone a lot smoother if she still had that warm afterglow rather than the frigid shoulder she'd given him.

Damn! Worrying about it wouldn't do any good. They'd straighten everything out tomorrow when they met for their regular session. Icy fingers of dread clutched his insides. Assuming she didn't cancel.

HATE HAD ALWAYS SEEMED like such a strong word to Emma. But she honestly thought she just might hate Nick Ryder's guts. Thanks to him, her life was going straight down the tubes. Her thesis was in serious jeopardy, and now so was her waitressing job after demolishing over a dozen glasses and ticking off two customers so much that they actually got up and walked out of the pub. And left *her* with their unpaid check.

She probably should have cancelled today's session with Nick, she thought as she pulled into the lab parking lot. Facing him so soon tied her stomach up in knots. But until she forced him to confess to the moronic stunt he'd pulled, and failing that, call him on it, she wouldn't be able to get back on track with her thesis.

Assuming that were possible.

She bit her lip. God, it had to be. She'd run out of money and time.

Damn him. Damn him. Damn him.

She parked and hurried around to the front of the lab. By the time she unlocked the door, out of the corner of her eye, she caught a glimpse of his red Porsche pulling into the lot.

What the hell was he doing here already? She'd purposely come early so that she had time to change and then compose herself, rehearse what she was going to say. She had a good mind to lock him out until she was good and ready.

But that would defeat her plan for getting him to spill his guts. She had to let him think nothing was wrong. After the way she left him last night, did she ever have her work cut out for her.

She left the door unlocked and hurried to get things ready. Instead of changing, she shrugged out of her coat and put her usual oversized white shirt over her uniform, and then slid on a pair of jeans. It took a few deep knee bends and some wiggling to stuff herself and her uniform in the already tight jeans, but she managed to get zipped seconds before he opened the door.

"Hi," she said, casually, even though the sight of him alone broke her heart. "You're early."

"Yeah." He lifted a shoulder and paid special attention to closing the door. When he faced her again, his eyes were wary and tired. "I figured we needed extra time to talk."

"I suppose we do." She cleared her throat. "I'm sorry about the way I acted—"

"No, it was me. I pushed too hard." He rubbed the back of his neck, blew out a breath. "I'm sorry. I really am. I don't want to ruin our relationship."

"What relationship?" It took all her nerve to ask, even though it shouldn't matter anymore.

Wariness crawled over his face. "Our professional one, of course," he said, and she had to bite her tongue to keep from lashing out at him. "But more important we're friends."

She pressed her lips together. He had an odd notion of friendship. In her book, friends didn't screw each other. And he sure had. Unfortunately, her only possible hope of completing her thesis in time depended upon him. The idea galled her.

She forced a smile. "Don't worry, Nick. Everything is fine. No hard feelings?" She stuck out her hand.

Judging by the stunned look on his face, she might as well have hauled off and slapped him. He ignored her outstretched hand and raised his gaze to hers, having the incredible nerve to look hurt.

She withdrew her hand and rounded her desk to her chair. Her legs were a little shaky and she didn't trust them to hold up. "Shall we get started?"

He muttered a curse.

"Excuse me?"

He sat in his usual seat in moody silence, shoving his hand through his hair, clenching and unclenching his jaw.

"Let's see." She consulted her notebook, not seeing a thing, but trying like hell to gather her thoughts together.

"Emma?"

She looked up with arched brows.

"We have to talk."

She gave a dismissive laugh. "We just did."

"I have something to tell you." His expression was grim, his posture tense. "It won't be particularly pleasant."

Oh, God. She wasn't ready. Not yet. She blinked. Maybe he wanted to tell her something else—like how he wanted to only be friends, make sure she understood there were no promises, no future.

It didn't matter. There wasn't a damn thing he could say that she wanted to hear. But when they did discuss the despicable way he'd deceived her, she wanted it to be on her terms. She wanted to show him how frustrating it was to feel helpless, to be at someone else's mercy.

She pasted a look of innocent concern on her face. "You're not telling me you're dropping out of the study with only three more days to go, are you?"

"No, of course not."

She breathed an audible sigh of relief. "Thank God. I can't tell you how horrifying that would be for me. This thesis is my ticket to the real world, a better job. I'm so grateful you've stepped in, Nick."

At least he had the good grace to look away and shift uncomfortably. The jerk.

"The last couple of days it's really sunk in how important my participation is and—"

She held up a hand. "I know, Nick. And I really appreciate you. Let's go ahead with our session."

"Whatever you want, Emma, it's your show." He slumped back, looking unsettled.

It sure as hell will be.

The smell of triumph tamped down some of her nervousness.

"Don't get too comfortable," she said in what she hoped was a teasing tone. "We'll be doing something a little different today."

His gaze narrowed. "What?"

She inclined her head toward the recliner in the corner. "Remember you asked me what we used that chair for? Today you're going to find out."

He looked far from thrilled. "Are you going to hook me up to that machine?"

"What's the matter, Nick, don't you trust me?"

"Of course I do."

"It's just a lie detector."

His gaze flew to her as if she were crazy.

"I'm kidding, come on." She laughed and stood. He didn't. "I'll explain what I'm doing as we go along."

Exhaling sharply, he pushed himself up.

"Go get comfortable while I get some water. Or maybe you'd prefer a shot of tequila?"

He froze.

She laughed. "I'm kidding. This won't be bad at all. Go sit."

As soon as she got to the back room she sank against the counter to steady herself. If she weren't so damn nervous and angry and hurt she could be enjoying this. But the most tragic thing of all was that it was still difficult to ignore his killer grin, or gaze into his whiskey-brown eyes and not want to make excuses for him. Rationalize what he'd done.

What kind of damn fool did that make her?

Anger surged and overtook the hurt and nervousness. Her plan was perfect. He wouldn't be in any position to try and charm anyone, much less persuade her that he wasn't a snake on two legs. She grabbed two bottles of Evian and returned with new resolve.

That he was sitting tentatively at the edge of the recliner, his feet still on the floor, his expression wary, gave her some satisfaction.

"I told you to get comfortable." She passed him his bottle, and bit her lip when his warm fingers brushed her hand.

"Put your feet up, lie back," she ordered, and then quickly turned away.

He did as she asked with reluctance in every move he made. She hoped he didn't give her a hassle about the next step. If he felt the least bit guilty over what he'd done, he probably wouldn't, but the possibility remained that he didn't have a conscience. That he didn't care one whit about her.

The thought cut her so deeply she wanted to drop everything and run for her car. Screw him. Screw her thesis. Hell, she was already screwed. But that would be too easy on him.

When she faced him again, he was laying back, his legs stretched out, his arms resting at his sides, his eyes boring directly into hers. She started to lift his arm onto the armrest, but decided against the physical contact.

Sadly, it was difficult enough being this close to him. Feeling his heat, smelling his musky masculine scent, remembering the intimacies they had shared last night.

Damn him.

She swallowed around the lump in her throat, and patted the armrest. "Put your arms here."

He slowly obeyed but snatched back his arm when she slipped a scarf around it. "What's that for?"

"I thought it would be easier on your wrists than the leather strap."

His gaze darted from the scarf in her hand, to her face and then to the machine. "Why do I need to be tied down?"

"So you won't jerk when I use the electric shock on you."

He sat up.

She gave his chest a none-too-gentle shove to make him recline again. "I'm kidding. Where's your sense of humor?"

He gave her a funny look that told her she needed to cool it or she'd blow everything.

"I'm going to tie these scarves very loosely around your wrists so that while you're in a dream state you won't—"

His bark of laughter cut her off. "I hate to rain on your parade but there is no way I'll be able to fall asleep here."

"When Brenda first suggested you as a subject, she said you're able to sleep anywhere."

"That's generally true, but—"

"Let's give it a try. This is an important part of my research."

He sighed, eyed the scarf again. "Is that really necessary?"

She gave him a seductive smile. "And here I thought the idea might excite you."

His entire expression changed. He went from hesitant to interested in half a heartbeat, the corners of his mouth already curving. "I'm all yours."

Men were so easy. Steer their mind in the direction of sex and they were putty—*silly* putty, in her opinion. She smiled as sweetly as she could and tied the first scarf, careful not to bind him too tightly and spook him. Although now that he was thinking with his other head, she probably could get away with quite a bit.

The second scarf she tied more securely, which didn't seem to faze him. He was still watching her with that stupid grin on his face. Okay, so it wasn't stupid. It was still sexy but that didn't mean she'd let it get to her.

She went around to the first arm and yanked the scarf tighter. He did react then, jerking and sending her a suspicious look, but it was too late. He wasn't going to get up until she let him up.

"Ready?" she asked brightly.

His response was more of a grunt than a yes.

"Okay." She took her time, returning to her desk to get her notebook and pencil, before sitting on the chair beside him. "Comfortable?"

He narrowed his gaze, but then it went to her mouth and his face relaxed. His gaze lingered, making her a little edgy. "Just fine."

She wanted to scoot her chair back. She didn't like being this close even if he was tied down. But she'd be damned if she'd show a single sign of weakness.

"Now, before I try to induce sleep, I'll explain—"

"Back up." He tensed. "Induce sleep?"

She nodded, presenting a picture of innocence.

"You're gonna swing a ball in front of my face, or something?"

"Or something."

His frown deepened. "Like hypnosis?"

She gave a noncommittal shrug, but didn't even try to sound convincing. "I wouldn't call it that."

"You'd better tell me what you call it because I know that a subject has to be willing for hypnosis to work."

"Don't worry." She smiled. "Anyway, as I was saying—"

He started rotating his left wrist as if he were trying to work it free.

"Is it too tight?"

"Yeah, a little."

"I'm sorry." She leaned across him and yanked it tighter.

When the expected protest didn't come she sat back and eyed him with suspicion.

She realized immediately what had distracted him. Her blouse had puckered open and the top of her red satin uniform was showing. What little there was of it. He was getting a bird's-eye view of the tops of her breasts.

Amazingly her face didn't turn several shades of pink. Even when she settled back and noticed the bulge forming beneath his fly, perversely, she decided not to straighten her blouse. Let him suffer.

Unfortunately, the new development did little for her concentration. She took a sip of water and recalled the predicament she was in because of him, the humiliation she felt over having believed his stupid stories. That helped get her back on track.

"Okay, we're going to be doing something a little different today."

He met her understatement with an incredulous look. "Wait. Before we get started, I have a question."

"Sure."

"What are you wearing under that shirt?"

She blinked in surprise. She was really getting this innocent act down pat. "What?" She glanced down, and opened her shirt a little more. "This? It's my uniform."

"Uniform?" The startled confusion on his face was almost comical.

"You know I work as a waitress, right?"

"Yeah, but—"

He stopped abruptly when she undid the top two buttons and exposed more of the red satin, and her mounding breasts. "I still haven't decided if I like it yet. The color and material are fine, but it's…well… the style is rather skimpy for my taste."

He noisily cleared his throat. "It is a good color on you."

That nearly sent her into a fit of laughter. Nick Ryder at a loss for words and looking as helpless as a baby. Imagine.

"Thanks. So let's get started." She cocked her head to the side. "Nick?"

His gaze hadn't made it to her face yet. "Can I see the rest of it?"

"Do you always have such a one-track mind?"

"Absolutely. Which is why we should get the unveiling out of the way." He gave her *that grin*.

This time it did nothing for her. "Sorry, business comes first."

His eyes lit with hope. Did he think that after their session they'd continue where they left off last night? Was he ever in for a surprise.

"So that you understand what we're doing here today, I'm going to tell you about one of my dreams," she said with a perfectly straight face as he studied her with a sudden fascinated curiosity. "And then I'll explain what I think it means so you can get the idea of where we're going with all this."

He looked relieved and definitely interested as he relaxed back with a smile.

Just to shake things up a bit, she played with the front of her shirt, finally undoing another button. "Is it hot in here, or is it me?"

15

NICK WATCHED HER fan herself, blow air down the front of her shirt. It wasn't hot in the least, but he'd be damned if he'd admit it.

What the hell was up with her today? This wasn't Emma. Even when she was trying to be Doc she'd fallen short. She was edgy one minute, shy and tentative, but with a glint of determination in her eye the next. Was she paying him back for last night? That was all right. He could handle this kind of torture.

Twisting his wrists, he tested the strength of the scarves. He wasn't going anywhere. The hardness beneath his fly was another matter. The sucker was headed for the stars. And lying here like this, there was no hiding it.

"Nick, would you mind if I took—" She shook her head. "Never mind. That wouldn't be professional."

He laughed, choked. "I swear I wouldn't mind."

"Really?"

"Positive."

"Thanks. I'll only be two minutes." She smiled, and then walked over to her desk and picked up the phone.

He craned his neck to see her. "What are you doing?"

"Making a call. You said you didn't mind if I took a quick break."

"I thought you were—" He stopped himself. She knew damn well what he'd thought. No way would he give her the satisfaction of confirming it. He laid his head back down and waited for her to check her answering machine.

When she returned to the seat beside him, he asked, "You have a hot date tonight?"

In answer, she gave him an enigmatic smile that could go either way. He'd been joking, not expecting any kind of affirmative answer. The idea that she could have a date hit him like a heavyweight's punch.

That reaction was enough to make him crazy. Tiffany, Pamela, Kelly, all the women he dated went out with other guys. Not only did Nick not give a rat's ass, he encouraged them. But the thought of Emma with someone else, laughing and whispering, touching, kissing, made Nick want to break something. Anything.

"Okay, here goes." She curled one of her legs under her. "In my dream I met this guy. He had dark hair, dark eyes, was extremely intelligent, had a great sense of humor, a good job, a family he respected and who respected him, an all-around charming guy. The type most girls actually daydream about. Unfortunately, he knew it."

Unease crawled up his spine. He stared into her eyes but she gave nothing away. "Question."

"Yes?"

"Did you know this guy?"

She wrinkled her nose. "Let's say I had a vague sense of who he was."

Man, did he want to ask the obvious question. But she probably would have told him if he was the one in her dream, wouldn't she? No way he'd ask. He didn't need to be retrained to hear her dream. She was playing some sort of game and expected him to rise to the bait. Instead, he waited silently for her to continue.

She leaned back in her chair and toyed with her second button, allowing him brief glances of red satin and creamy skin. "Let's see…oh, yes…this guy asked me to meet with him one day, and I agreed. I wasn't sure about him at first. He was too charming, too sure of himself, and others did warn me about him.

"But I was pretty sure of myself, too, and couldn't imagine he would mean trouble for me. I was too sensible, too focused on where I wanted to go and how to get there."

She stopped. "I'm sorry. You're probably dying of thirst. I'll get your water."

"No, go on."

Ignoring him, she went to get the Evian still sitting on her desk. When she took too long, he twisted as far as he could to see what she was doing. Her back was to him, but it looked as though she was just standing there.

"Emma?"

She straightened, and he thought he heard a sniffle. "Coming."

Dread and guilt tangled in his gut. He strained against his bindings. They wouldn't give.

She came around the chair, smiling, and looking

perfectly normal. "This is going to be a little tricky. We don't want your shirt drenched."

Was he going crazy? Or was guilt doing a number on him? Making him see things that weren't there. "I'm okay. Let's get back to the dream."

She frowned, as though trying to solve a problem. "Here, bring your head up."

"You could untie me while I listen to your dream." He glanced at his bound wrist. "This hardly seems necessary for now."

"True." She thought for a moment. "I should have waited but this won't take long."

He was about to protest again, but she cupped the back of his neck with her soft hand and got so close he could smell her almond shampoo. Half sitting as he was, her breasts pressed lightly against his arm as she tipped the bottle up for him to take a drink.

When she drew back, he caught another glimpse of red satin and lots of cleavage. He lifted his gaze to her face and she smiled, a bit brazenly, which wasn't Emma's style.

"Had enough?" she asked, so sweetly, so innocently, he didn't know what to think anymore.

He nodded, and then watched as she returned to her chair and curled her legs up in an almost protective position.

"Okay." She frowned in thought, her gaze wandering out the window. "Do you remember where I left off?"

Her voice was casual. The way she suddenly looked pointedly at him was not.

"You met this guy who you were warned about,

but you didn't take the warnings seriously because you thought you were immune."

"Ah, yes." The sudden flash of anger in her eyes was not his imagination. In the next second, she looked perfectly calm again. "But I underestimated him and this illusive appeal he was supposed to have. Not only was he extremely charming but he was sly. He made me believe he wanted to help me." Her voice faltered. She blinked a couple of times, and then moistened her lips. "He made me think I just might be special."

He opened his mouth for the second time...not a damned thing came out.

"I could handle that...um...miscommunication. Not that I wasn't hurt by it. Of course I was hurt and angry. But he'd also led me to believe that I could count on him. But he lied, and left me hanging out to dry." Her gaze pierced his, her eyes stark with misery and contempt. "And that hurt most of all."

"Emma, please untie me. I can explain."

"What's the matter, Nick? It's just a dream. A sketchy part of reality...almost a fantasy. Can't you tell the difference?"

"Please, Emma." He jerked his wrists but the scarves didn't loosen. "Let me explain."

She folded her arms across her chest. "Go ahead."

"Untie me."

"You can explain from right there."

Nick inhaled deeply. His throat was tight. How the hell had she found out? "I was going to tell you last night." Her eyebrows rose. "I swear. I know I was a jerk, but I didn't really know you a week ago."

"Let me make sure I understand this." She cocked

her head to the side with nonchalance. But he'd already seen the pain and anger in her eyes, so dark and deep he could drown in it. "Because you don't know someone, it's okay to screw with their career? To sabotage a project they'd worked on for over a year?"

"That's not what I'm saying." He jerked his wrist and got nowhere. "I didn't want to do the study. Brenda coerced me—" He sighed with disgust. "That's not true. She had something I wanted and we made a deal. If I reneged, I lost. If you threw me out of the study, that would be different...."

She let silence lapse. "That's an explanation?"

He closed his eyes, no longer able to face the sadness in hers.

"It's an excuse, Nick, not an explanation," she said, her voice so soft, he barely heard her.

"Emma, it seemed harmless at the time. I didn't think." God, he hated feeling this helpless. "I'm really sorry." A thought struck him. "You saw the magazines last night."

She didn't say anything. She didn't have to. Fresh pain entered her bleak stare.

He wanted to wrap his arms around her, promise her everything would be all right. Dammit, he'd make it all right. "Will you please untie me?"

She slowly shook her head. "Want to hear the end of the dream?" When he didn't answer, she said, "I think you get the picture."

With a heartbreakingly sad face, she turned and headed for her desk.

An expression he'd remember for one hell of a long time. "What are you doing now?"

Ignoring him, she cleared off her desk, locked it, and then walked past him into the back room.

"Emma, you can't leave me here like this." Shit! What he did was wrong, but how mature was she being? "Emma!"

She appeared again after several minutes, her purse in hand. Although she seemed fairly composed, her eyes were red.

"I know you're angry. I don't blame you. But we need to talk about this."

Indecision and resentment warred in her face as she stood staring at him, her keys already dangling from her fingers.

"Emma," he said in a soothing voice, "be rational."

She blinked in surprise. And then glared in outrage. "You don't think I'm being rational?"

"Hey, it's me. I don't think, remember?" He didn't even get a ghost of a smile out of her. "I didn't mean anything. I'm just trying to get some dialogue going so we can fix this thing."

"Yeah, you're real good with dialogue," she mumbled, her expression tight and unyielding.

He didn't say a word, just watched with relief as she loosened one of his hands. Not all the way, but he'd be able to work his way out of the silk noose.

"Thanks, Em, I knew you'd be reasonable," he said as she walked around to the other side. Except she didn't stop. She kept on walking. "You forgot to untie my other hand."

She got to the door and turned for a second and said, "You're resourceful, figure it out."

"Wait...there's more."

The door slammed behind her.

Nick let out a string of curses that would make a sailor blush.

BY THE TIME SHE GOT to her car, Emma's hands were shaking so badly that she couldn't get the key in the lock. She took several deep breaths, trying to calm down. She had to get out of here before he freed himself. They had nothing more to say to each other.

Too bad her plan had fallen apart. But halfway through her act, she couldn't think about anything but getting the hell out of there and away from him. It didn't matter. She'd gotten the point across. And without blubbering like an idiot. That was something.

She sniffed, dabbed at her watery eyes, and then attacked the lock. This time the key slid in and she hurriedly got behind the wheel. The ignition was a little trickier placed below the steering wheel as it was, but she managed to work the key in and get the engine started while shooting glances toward the entrance.

It was probably stupid and arrogant of her to think he'd even try to follow. More likely she'd never see him again. He had enough women waiting in the wings. Ones who didn't care that he was a low-down, conniving snake. Better he stay out of her life. God only knew she had enough problems ahead of her trying to salvage her thesis.

She realized she'd been sitting at the edge of the street, waiting for a chance to pull out, except there was no traffic.

She cursed to herself and glanced in the rearview mirror. No sign of him.

Why should that surprise her? He probably couldn't even see how wrong he'd been to pass off those disgusting stories as his dreams. He was probably too busy patting himself on the back for being so clever. What a jerk!

The look on his face when recognition dawned flashed in her mind. No, he knew he was wrong. Horribly wrong. That by no means excused him.

A honking horn made her jump and she realized she'd gone through a red light. Great. She checked the rearview mirror. No cop. No Nick, either.

What the hell was wrong with her? She didn't want him to follow. She really didn't. Confrontation was something she tried to avoid. Anything he said would make matters worse, anyway. She'd abandoned the idea of asking him to help her reconstruct the time and dreams they'd lost. It wouldn't work. Not only did she not trust him, she didn't want him around reminding her of what a fool she'd been.

Brenda had warned her. Why couldn't she have listened? She was as arrogant as Nick, that's why. No man would ever get to her or interfere in her life. What a joke. She'd practically wrapped herself up in a package with a big bow. God, she'd been easy picking.

Especially for someone as astute and charming as Nick.

It hurt like hell to think of him. To picture that sexy grin that always made her knees weak...those dark seductive eyes, full of intelligence and humor...that mouth of his, how it knew just what her body wanted.

Lust. That's all it was. She'd been a victim of lust

more than anything else. The idea made her feel marginally better. Nick was a good-looking guy with a great body and very skillful hands. She was a healthy young woman. Why wouldn't she have been interested?

Who the hell was she kidding?

The light didn't turn yellow until she reached the intersection, but she stopped anyway, thankful for the couple of minutes to pull herself together without being a menace. Her head spun with self-disgust and anger at Nick and herself and fear that she would never get her thesis done. She had no business being on the road.

After crossing the intersection, she pulled over to the side, crossed her wrists on the steering wheel and laid her forehead on them, eyes closed. Even if she had all the correct data, she was in no condition to complete the project. Her nerves were shot and her hard-earned ability to concentrate, her most crucial defense against certain failure would be put to the test. She honestly didn't know if she could handle it without ending up in a psych ward.

A bitter laugh escaped her. The irony was too much. Here she was supposed to be a psychologist and she couldn't even get her own act together.

And worst of all, she was going to miss Nick.

She took a couple of deep breaths before lifting her head. Blinking several times helped clear the haze of depression that was doing a number on her weary eyes. She looked around, amazed to realize she didn't know where she was.

But what the hell, she didn't know who she was anymore either.

16

FOR TWO DAYS Nick had felt like crap, the biggest heel east of the Mississippi, but now he was pissed.

Two days and he hadn't heard from her. He'd left a dozen messages on her answering machine, even drove past her apartment and the lab. Her car hadn't been at either place. So where was she? And why hadn't Brenda laid into him yet? Obviously Emma hadn't told her about what a dirtbag her brother was, because Brenda had never been shy about pointing out when he screwed up.

The worst part was she'd always been a confidant if he needed one. They'd been close since their teen years when he'd decked Billy Werner for making a nasty crack about Brenda's thighs, and she'd erased Nick's name and number off the girls' locker room wall. He would've rather she left the information there, but he knew she'd been well intentioned.

He sat in front of the TV, massaging his aching temple with one hand, a bottle of beer in the other, and not giving a crap if the Panthers beat the Vikings, even if it looked like they could go to the Super Bowl.

He couldn't talk to Brenda about this. She'd be more likely to help Emma dig his grave than lend support or advice. Of course he'd deserve it, but he also deserved a hearing. He needed to talk to Emma.

Hell, he needed to talk to somebody, before guilt ate him alive. Or before he drank himself silly, or started talking to the walls. Because the problem had gotten a lot worse, or at least more complicated than him being a horse's ass. He thought he might be falling in love with Emma.

God, he never thought that would happen. The idea scared the hell out of him. But it wouldn't go away. He missed her. He hurt because he'd hurt her. He thought of nothing or no one else but her. Did that all add up to love?

How was he supposed to know? No one had ever made him want to slay dragons before. Not that she'd asked. She'd only wanted him to honor his commitment, and he'd failed her.

He took another long pull of beer, tempted to drink himself into a stupor. But he'd disappointed her enough. Hell, he'd disappointed himself—a new experience for him. It sucked.

Leaning his head back, he stared at the ceiling instead of the TV. He didn't know what the score was, didn't care. Even though he had a bet with Marshall.

He brought his head up.

Marshall.

Nick could talk to him. He didn't have to cop to the whole sordid story but he could still get some feedback. In some ways, his friend was like Emma. Driven, focused, always knowing what he wanted to be, where he wanted to go in life. Everyone knew he'd marry Sally when they both graduated. That had been one of Marshall's goals.

He was the most dedicated family man Nick knew. His kids and wife meant everything to him, and he worked hard to give them a nice home and the kids a good education, yet he still made time for friends and tennis and football. The guy had it together, a totally balanced life. And he was happy.

Nick picked up the phone he'd set next to him in case she finally called, and he dialed Marshall's number. Maybe Nick had believed his own propaganda for too long. Maybe there actually was life after commitment.

"I HOPE I DIDN'T DRAG you away from some family thing," Nick said as soon as Marshall got a beer out of the fridge and came into the family room. "It's already the fourth quarter."

"Nah." Marshall sank into the burgundy leather couch and twisted off his beer cap. He looked tired. "Who's winning?"

Nick snorted. "Shit!"

Marshall laughed without humor. "I don't know what's going on either." He took a deep drink. "I'm glad you called."

Nick frowned at the seriousness in his voice. "What's up?"

Marshall shook his head and sighed. "I did something really stupid and it's eating at me."

Join the club. Nick nearly laughed out loud at the irony. Instead, he waited while his friend took another gulp.

"This is hard for me to admit." Marshall straightened from his slouched position, leaned forward, and rested his elbows on his thighs. He stared down at the carpet while he spoke. "I've been having an affair."

The words knocked the wind out of Nick. The world tipped precariously to the right. He tried not to react. He didn't even know what to say. Marshall was the last person he'd expected to do something that stupid.

"You look surprised."

"Nah." Nick shrugged. "Well, yeah, hell yeah I am. What happened?"

Marshall hung his head and stared hard at his tennis shoes. "I'm an ass. What can I say?"

"Does Sally know?"

"That I'm an ass?" A smile tugged at his friend's mouth. "She knew when she married me."

Nick chuckled, mostly because he was expected to, and Marshall didn't look like he needed anybody else beating up on him.

"She doesn't know. At least I don't think she does. Shit! It would serve me right if she found out." His eyes were bleak and scared when he turned to Nick. "God, I hope she never does. It would kill her."

"Is it over?" Nick asked quietly, still shocked, still not sure what to say.

Marshall nodded. "For over a month. The money I borrowed from you—" He stared down at his shoes again. "It was for an abortion."

"Geez."

"Yeah."

"The woman, is she okay with the breakup, or is that another problem?"

"The reason I borrowed so much money from you is that I sent her to Aruba to recover after the—" He closed his eyes and shook his head. "I never thought this could happen to me."

"Tell you the truth, pal, I didn't either." He winced at Marshall's shamed expression. "I only meant that you and Sally were *the* couple. You guys have been together forever, and I figured...I don't know..."

"Yeah." Marshall pointed his beer bottle at the wide-screen TV. "You caught the score yet?"

Nick laughed. "I can't even remember who's playing."

"Sorry to bum you out like this. I know how much you think of Sally."

"I'm not bummed." That was a blatant lie. If Marshall couldn't cut married life, stay committed, then Nick didn't stand a chance. He was bound to fail. "I wish there was something I could do."

"You already have. Keeping it inside was eating me alive." He gave Nick a wry smile. "I hate to admit it, pal, but you were right all along."

Nick didn't like how that sounded. "About?"

"Staying single. Sticking to the flavor of the week instead of having the whole damn gallon of ice cream at one time."

"You're tired of being married."

"Hell, no. I made a mistake, but I still love my wife. I hope Sally doesn't find out about Melanie and throw my sorry ass out into the street. I just wish I'd sowed a few wild oats after college instead of rushing into things. Maybe then I wouldn't have been so curious and flattered by Melanie's attention.'' His sigh was pure disgust. ''It sounds like I'm making excuses.''

''Don't we all.'' Nick got up to get them each another beer. Maybe he would drink himself into a stupor after all. Marshall. Of all guys.

''How've you been doing?'' Marshall asked, eyeing him with sudden interest. ''You don't look so hot yourself.''

''Me? Fine. Couldn't be better.'' He was the golden boy, wasn't he? Lots of money and women at his disposal, and not a care in the world. Until two days ago, when his entire life had gone straight to hell.

WHOEVER WAS AT THE DOOR wasn't going away. First two rounds of doorbell chimes, knocking and then the idiot started pounding. Nick knew it wasn't Emma, or he would have answered it right away. But it had been four days without a word from her.

For the sake of his headache and neighborhood peace, he opened the door.

''About damn time.'' Brenda pushed past him. ''What the hell is going on?''

Ignoring her, he returned to the couch, the wide screen and his lukewarm bottle of beer.

She picked up the remote control and turned off the tube. Big deal. He wasn't following the game anyway. ''Nick, you're going to talk to me.''

He grunted.

"What happened between you and Emma?"

"Get me a cold beer while you're up."

"I get that beer and it'll end up over your head." She sat beside him on the couch, concern creasing her face. "What's going on?"

"I'm sure Doc told you all about it."

"Emma won't say a word. She wouldn't even return my calls. I had to track her down."

That got his attention. "Where is she?"

Alarm flashed in her eyes. "Answer me first."

Two days ago, Nick would have told her to kiss his butt. But forty-eight hours of little sleep and too much thinking had knocked him down a peg. "Is she working on her thesis?"

"I don't think so. She's been working double shifts at the restaurant."

He groaned.

"Nick." She gently touched his arm. "Tell me."

He passed a hand over his face, cupped his mouth and blew into his palm. Sighing, he let his hand fall to his lap. "I screwed up, Bren. Bad. Really bad."

She said nothing, only stared at him with dread clouding her features.

"I did something that might have jeopardized her study." He shook his head in self-disgust. "*Has* jeopardized her study."

"On purpose?"

"Of course not." He sighed and rubbed the back of his neck. "Not really. It's complicated."

"What did you do, Nick?" Not a speck of sympathy in her eyes. Nor did he deserve any.

"You know I wasn't crazy about the whole thing

from the beginning, and a few days into the study, I thought I'd cleverly found a way to get thrown out.'' He winced inwardly at the angry disappointment in Bren's face. ''I figured you wouldn't penalize me if it was Emma's choice that I didn't continue.''

''What did you do?''

He explained about the magazines, his chest tightening as the look of disbelief on his sister's face turned to panic. Anger, loathing, contempt, any of those he could take, but not the fear and misery he saw growing.

She sank back, genuinely shaken. ''You have no idea what you've done.''

''I'm beginning to.''

''Emma is never going to finish her thesis on time.''

''She could if she—'' Brenda's grim shake of her head stopped him. ''Why not?''

''I think I told you about how Emma struggled with a learning disability while growing up.''

''Yeah, she mentioned it, too.''

''She did? That's unusual. She never tells anyone about that,'' Brenda said, her expression speculative.

Great. Emma had trusted him with something she held private and he turned around and screwed her. This kept getting better.

''She had a moderate case of dyslexia, which unfortunately wasn't detected right away. Her mother and teachers gave her a terrible time, accusing her of being lazy and stupid.''

He cringed at the thought of any child being subjected to that sort of abuse, but especially Emma.

"Yeah, I know," Brenda said, clearly in tune with his reaction. "Anyway, her mom worked with her, or I guess a better word would be badgered, but it was Emma who realized the only way she could overcome the handicap was to learn to concentrate. Really concentrate, keep totally focused. Only then did she begin transposing letters and numbers less and less."

"Isn't there medication or therapy or something for that sort of thing?"

"I don't know. But this was fifteen-twenty years ago in rural Utah, don't forget."

"And now?"

"She still has some trouble. It takes her longer than you or me to read anything. But she's a hard worker, so as long as she stays focused she's okay." Brenda's gaze held no condemnation, but she wasn't pulling any punches either.

He'd screwed up and she wanted him to own up to it.

He looked away, and muttered a pithy four-letter word. "The letters might have been made up but there's got to be some value in analyzing them. They're someone else's fantasies, just not mine." At least that's how he'd justified it at the time.

"Dreams and fantasies are two different things." Brenda gave him a measuring look. "You think Emma would compromise her study like that?"

He sighed. Of course she wouldn't. "Go ahead, kick my ass. I deserve it."

"That would be too easy."

"I feel like shit."

"You should." Jackson had jumped up on the

couch between them, and Brenda idly stroked his thick black coat. "What are you going to do about it?"

"She won't even talk to me."

"And that's stopping you? You're going to turn tail and run the first time something doesn't go your way or things get difficult?"

"That isn't fair. My life isn't perfect." He got up and headed to the kitchen for another beer.

Brenda followed. "It's not easy, is it? Feeling helpless and frustrated. Emma's felt that way most of her life. But she's not a quitter."

Now she was pissing him off. "Shut up, Bren. You don't know what you're talking about." He grabbed his beer and then shouldered past her.

She stayed on his heels. "Do you like Emma?"

He hesitated, thought about ignoring her, but he knew his sister too well. She wouldn't let up. "Of course I do."

"How much?"

"What kind of question is that?" The couch seat was dented where he'd camped out for the past four days. He sank back down and uncapped his beer.

Brenda sat right down next to him. "Do you like her but if you never saw her again it wouldn't matter? Or do you care what happens to her?"

"Yeah, I care what happens to her, dammit."

Brenda's lips turned up in a small grin.

He scowled at her. "What?"

"Maybe we could use a little stronger word than like?"

Nick took a deep breath. A funny feeling fluttered

in his chest. He took a big gulp of beer. "I don't know."

"Okay, that's honest."

He laid his head back, and closed his eyes. "She'd never once asked me for a damn thing."

"Not exactly. She asked you to participate in the study."

"You know what I mean. But thanks for rubbing it in."

Brenda's soft chuckle drew his attention. "I didn't mean to. I'm merely pointing out that all Emma wanted from you was your commitment to see the project through and—"

"And I failed her. Gee thanks, Bren, but I already figured that one out for myself and I'm not even a psych major."

"Since I am a psych major, let me finish." She poked his arm hard when he closed his eyes again.

"I'm listening."

"Even if you hated how the study was going, I know you too well, Nick Ryder, you would not screw it up."

"News flash. I did."

"I didn't get to the unless part." Her expression softened. "Unless you were scared."

"Right." He snorted. "Why didn't you major in French?"

"Maybe Emma started making you see life differently, made you start thinking about change and that scared the hell out of you."

"Now are you finished?"

She gave him a sad, disappointed look, and then nodded.

"Good." He sighed. Should he admit his dreams had turned to Emma and that's what prompted the magazine idea? "You may have a point." Her eyes lit up and she opened her mouth, but promptly shut it when he put up a hand.

He laid his head back again, thinking, grateful that Brenda respected his need for silence. Inside his head was a jumble of thoughts and emotions that made it hard to think. Guilt and shame were in there, for having screwed up Emma's project, and then guilt for simply having so much when others didn't.

Though that was nothing new, and he tried to make up for it through volunteer work. But Emma's personal struggles drove the inequity home. She was an amazing woman. With each layer of her personality that peeled away, she became more incredible. And dammit, he wanted to be there as the rest of the layers fell away. He wanted to be there for the long haul. If she'd let him.

"Bren, I have an idea that could fix everything." He looked into his sister's pleased face. "It may take a day or two and I might need your help."

EMMA TRUDGED into the back room of the lab, still lethargic after sleeping for most of yesterday. Nick had stopped leaving messages on her answering machine two days ago, so she was fairly confident he'd moved on and forgotten all about her by now.

The idea shouldn't hurt. If she had half a brain in her head she'd feel nothing but relief. But even before she started studying psychology she knew love and logic often couldn't occupy the same space.

Oh, God, she had to quit thinking about him, quit convincing herself that she'd fallen in love. She hadn't even known him long enough. On top of that, he'd made a fool out of her. How could she possibly have any feelings for him at all?

Love was only a state of mind. By next week she'd have moved on, too. After some of the pain subsided. Time did help heal. She had experience in that area. But right now, it hurt so damn bad.

She stared into the small refrigerator, wondering what she'd been looking for. And then she remembered. Evian. For Brenda, who would be meeting her at any minute. But since Emma hadn't been in for the past five days the fridge was nearly bare. Two other psych grad students used the place, too, but they rarely remembered to replenish anything.

She took out a carton of yogurt that had been there awhile and lifted the top. Immediately she held it at arm's length until she got to the small sink. She didn't have to sniff it to know it should have been pitched weeks ago.

It took a while for the sluggish stream of water to rinse out the carton, and she idly stared, wondering what was so urgent that Brenda insisted on meeting her here this afternoon. Not this evening or tomorrow, but this afternoon. When Emma had tried to put her off, Brenda had called in every favor, even tried shaming Emma into meeting with her.

The shaming ploy had worked. It wasn't Brenda's

fault her brother was a snake...charming, good-looking, funny, but still a snake.

Oh, God, here she was thinking about him again.

"I'm not going to do that," she said out loud. "I'm not going to do that."

She finished rinsing out the disgusting yogurt, which probably would have made a great science project, and turned off the faucet. Without the noise from the running water, she heard something in the outer lab. Was it the door opening?

"Brenda?"

No answer.

"Brenda?" Emma cautiously poked her head through the door. No one was there. She laughed at herself for being so jumpy, and then saw the large binder on the desk. It wasn't hers, and it hadn't been there earlier.

She peered out the window before going to have a look. The parking lot was deserted.

Uneasy, she stared at the binder...large, black and totally unfamiliar. Odd. Of course one of the other students could have left it, but she would have noticed it before...

When she realized she was approaching it as though it might explode she had to laugh at herself. Until she saw the folded paper with her name in bold black letters. That definitely hadn't been there earlier. She hesitated, trying to figure out if she recognized the writing. Not a clue.

Tentatively she picked up the piece of paper. Nothing was written inside, however, on top of the binder was a small tape cassette. She hadn't even unlocked her drawer yet, and as she fumbled with her key, trying to get to her recorder, she flipped open the binder.

The top page read, *Dreams by Nick Ryder*. She immediately sank to her chair. The next page was an index of dates and dreams going back to their third session. She flipped through the next fifty pages. There were narratives, diagrams, and charts on feelings, written in the style of a journal. There were at least another fifty pages of the same, all neatly typed in chronological order with incredible detail.

How could this be? Had he kept notes all along? Was this another made-up batch of fantasies?

She leaned back and started to read the first narrative. When she neared the end, and referenced the journal entries, she realized the dream was about her. So were the next night's recording, and the one after that. On one date, there was no entry, but the simple statement—no dreams, sleepless night. It was the night of his reception, where under the moon beside the pond, everything had shifted between them.

Over two hours later when her neck and shoulder muscles started to cramp, she realized she'd read nonstop. Nick had put an incredible amount of thought and work into providing so much detail, but more importantly, he'd really laid himself open.

She swallowed, knowing how much he hated being this exposed, but he'd done it. To make amends, assuage his guilt, she reminded herself. This wasn't about her.

Or was it?

Her gaze riveted to the first page. His dreams told a different story. She couldn't ignore them. The dark-haired mystery woman in his dreams—he'd figured out who she was by the third night. He thought she was Emma.

A shiver ran down her spine.

She had to clear her head and concentrate. Be objective. What a joke.

She leaned back in her chair, trying to compose herself, and saw the tape. She'd forgotten about it. Quickly she slipped it into her recorder. The sound of Nick's voice sent her pulse into overdrive. She closed her eyes and rested her head back while she listened.

"I'm sending this because I figured you wouldn't talk to me," he was saying. "I only hope that no matter how you feel about me right now, you'll believe and use this information. I recorded my dreams each morning after so this isn't from memory. It's all fresh and accurate. And Emma, if you never want to see me again, I'll respect your wishes."

She kept her eyes closed, letting the tape continue, even though it appeared he'd had nothing more to say. He'd actually dreamt of her, and it had scared him. It was still no excuse for what he'd done but...

"I lied."

At the sound of his voice again she jumped and opened her eyes. It wasn't coming from the tape. Nick was standing in the doorway, unshaven, dark circles under his eyes, his hair a mess, clothes wrinkled, as though he hadn't slept for days.

He gave her a lopsided grin. "Don't worry. I did shower and brush my teeth."

Emma's breath stalled in her chest. She cleared her throat. "What did you lie about?"

He shook his head as he came toward her. "If you don't want to see me, I can't respect your wishes."

"No?" She tensed as he got closer, not knowing if she should stay put or run like hell.

"Nope." He came around her desk, swiveled her chair so that she faced him. "I'm going to keep coming after you until you admit we're good for each other."

"But Nick—"

He pulled her up into his arms and then forced her chin up. "I was going to tell you I love you on the tape, but you'd just call me on it and tell me how chicken I am."

"But..." She blinked. Did he say...? "Love?"

"I knew you'd figure it out from my dreams, but I also figured you'd want to hear it from me." One side of his mouth lifted. "I love you, Doc." He kissed her gently, briefly. "You're going to have to tell me how it happened, because I sure can't figure it out."

"Nick...I..."

"What, Emma?" His expression turned serious. "Tell me."

She swallowed. "Okay, I love you, too."

He laughed. "Gee, I'm convinced."

"You're getting off too easy."

"I know." He kissed the tip of her nose. "On second thought, I never worked so hard for anything in my life."

She smiled against his suddenly eager mouth, and then gasped when he slid his hand up her shirt. He pushed her bra up to expose her breast and then cupped her heated flesh, while deepening the kiss.

"God, I've missed you," he whispered against her mouth, his arousal confirmation as it pressed against her belly. He slid his free hand down her back and worked his way under her waistband until he palmed her buttocks, pulling her hard against him.

She moaned softly, wishing they could rip off their clothes and lie naked together. She managed to get her hands under his shirt and then went straight for his belt buckle. He pushed his hips against her, his breath coming ragged and quick.

A second later he stiffened. She froze, confused, and he slowly slid his hand out of her pants. He gave her breast a gentle squeeze, and then pulled her bra back into place.

"We're going to have to put this on hold," he said, his voice filled with regret. "I think we have company." He kissed the side of her mouth, drew in her lower lip between his teeth.

Emma thought she heard something. The door?

"Yes!"

They both turned to the voice coming from the doorway. Brenda pumped her arm in the air, a big grin on her face.

Emma automatically moved back, feeling like a kid who'd just reached into the cookie jar. And then she realized her friend looked *happy*. "Brenda?"

Nick smiled at his sister and pulled Emma back into his arms. "And you thought I was the sly one in the family."

"What's going on?"

Brenda sauntered in, and slid a hip onto the corner of the desk. "Did I ever tell you I changed the topic of my thesis?"

Emma slowly shook her head.

"It's called *Forbidden Fruit*."

Emma frowned, not understanding at first, and then it dawned on her. All the warnings about Nick. Her gaze flew to him. "You knew about this?"

"Not until last night."

She glared at Brenda. "You used us as guinea pigs?"

Brenda's grin widened. "Isn't it wonderful?"

Emma's mouth dropped open. She didn't know what to say.

"I think it is," Nick said, and Brenda sighed when his mouth covered Emma's.

Epilogue

Two years later

DEAR *MIDNIGHT FANTASY*,

I never thought I'd be writing a letter to a magazine like this but I wanted to tell you about how I met my husband. It all started with my wacky sister-in-law who thought we'd be the perfect match....

*H*ugh Blake,
soon to become stepfather to
the Maitland clan, has produced three
high-performing offspring of his own. But
at the rate they're going, they're never going to
make him a grandpa!

There's *Suzanne*, a work-obsessed CEO whose Christmas spirit
could use a little topping up....

And *Thomas*, a lawyer whose ability to hold on to the woman
he loves is evaporating by the minute....

And *Diane*, a teacher so dedicated to her teenage students she
hasn't noticed she's put her own life on hold.

But there's a Christmas wake-up call in store
for the Blake siblings. Love *and* Christmas miracles
are in store for all three!

Maitland Maternity Christmas

A collection from three of Harlequin's favorite authors

Muriel Jensen
Judy Christenberry
&Tina Leonard

Look for it in November 2001.

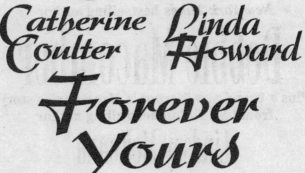

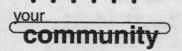

CALL THE ONES YOU LOVE OVER THE HOLIDAYS!

Save $25 off future book purchases when you buy any four Harlequin® or Silhouette® books in October, November and December 2001,

PLUS

receive a phone card good for 15 minutes of long-distance calls to anyone you want in North America!

WHAT AN INCREDIBLE DEAL!

Just fill out this form and attach 4 proofs of purchase (cash register receipts) from October, November and December 2001 books, and Harlequin Books will send you a coupon booklet worth a total savings of $25 off future purchases of Harlequin® and Silhouette® books, AND a 15-minute phone card to call the ones you love, anywhere in North America.

Please send this form, along with your cash register receipts as proofs of purchase, to:
In the USA: Harlequin Books, P.O. Box 9057, Buffalo, NY 14269-9057
In Canada: Harlequin Books, P.O. Box 622, Fort Erie, Ontario L2A 5X3
Cash register receipts must be dated no later than December 31, 2001.
Limit of 1 coupon booklet and phone card per household.
Please allow 4-6 weeks for delivery.

I accept your offer! Please send me my coupon booklet and a 15-minute phone card:

Name: _____

Address: _____ City: _____

State/Prov.: _____ Zip/Postal Code: _____

Account Number (if available): _____

---

097 KJB DAGL

PHQ4012

Harlequin Romance®
Love affairs that
last a lifetime.

HARLEQUIN *Presents*
Seduction and passion
guaranteed.

Harlequin®
® *Historical*
Historical
Romantic
Adventure.

HARLEQUIN®
Temptation.
Sassy, sexy, seductive!

HARLEQUIN® *Super*ROMANCE®
Emotional,
exciting,
unexpected.

HARLEQUIN®
AMERICAN *Romance*®
Heart, home
& happiness.

HARLEQUIN®
Duets™
Romantic comedy.

HARLEQUIN®
INTRIGUE®
Breathtaking
romantic suspense.

HARLEQUIN® *Blaze*™
Red-Hot Reads.

HARLEQUIN®
Makes any time special ®